A LISTING

OF THE WORKS OF

ROBERT NATHAN

WILL BE FOUND AT THE END

OF THIS VOLUME

THE FAIR

The FAIR

BY

ROBERT NATHAN

NEW YORK

Alfred · A · Knopf

1968

L. C. catalog card number: 64–12322

THIS IS A BORZOI BOOK,
PUBLISHED BY ALFRED A. KNOPF, INC.

Published April 1964
Second Printing, June 1968

To Minnie, with love

AUTHOR'S NOTE

This is not an accurate history, as far as I know. Still, there was a Celtic Prince, or King, named Arthur; and battles at Badon Hill and Salisbury Plain. And there were Saxons; and some people believed in wyverns and sorcerers and still do; and some people believed in angels.

This is man's life, and of his life the whole:
This yellow light of day, this little rose,
These clouds and dews and rivers where they roll,
This air of earth which all about him flows.
The hills and mountains and the watching snows,
The quiet ocean draining on her shore—
These he will view but once before he goes,
These when he leaves them he will see no more.
Let him be humble, arrogant or vain,
Let him be poor or cradled in his worth,
This beauty that will never come again,
This little heaven that we call the earth,
Is made to bloom by kindness and men's love
But only once, that I have knowledge of.

THE FAIR

CHAPTER 1

In those days, heaven was closer to earth, much of which still lay in darkness. But in the monasteries of Gaul, and in the west, the monks of St. Augustine and of St. Benedict labored over their parchments, illuminating with loving care the story of the Creation. Saints roamed the countryside, performing miracles, and it was said that angels had been seen descending to earth, which was flat, and suspended in space by God's will.

Yet, in the deep oak and beech forests of Britain, wizards and enchanters still flourished. And the thought of basilisks and other frightful beasts terrified the Celtic children at home behind the turf walls of their farmsteads, or in the stone forts and keeps left behind them by the Romans.

There, instructed by the good Fathers, the Priors and Abbots of the monasteries, the children of the Cymri studied Holy Writ, both in Latin and in the ancient tongue of the people, the multiplication of sums, the disposition of the heavenly bodies, and the lives of the martyrs.

It was the beginning of the Dark Ages, a time of sorrow and terror in the world. The works of the philosophers and historians of the past were no longer read; even the names of those who had been eagerly discussed in their own generation were forgotten. And men who in the days of the Roman Empire would have studied how to live with elegance, sought only the means to live at all, either on earth, or, failing that, in heaven.

In Britain the war horns of the Saxons were heard by the Brigantes and the Iceni, and the smoke of burning farmsteads and hamlets stained the air of the eastern shires. The horn-hatted hordes of Hengist, the Jute, harried the country south to Devonshire, and west to Severnside.

Fighting for their hearths and homes, the Celtic chieftains, many of whom had Roman blood in their veins, united under Arthur, a Prince of the Cymri. In the long years that followed, Arthur won a great victory at Badon Hill; it was but one victory in a war which seemed endless. The Saxon tide ebbed and flowed across the land; Hengist died and was replaced by Cerdic, and Arthur rode out to battle year after year.

Now, old and wearied, and in trouble with his wife, Gwenifer, he was riding out for the last time, to Salisbury Plain. With him went Modred, who some said was his son by blood, and Lord Morven of Thane, whose own young son, Godwin, and niece, Penrhyd, were at that moment sitting at lessons in their schoolroom at home, along with Odo, the Abbot of Swynneddfod, their teacher.

Penrhyd at fifteen was a slender girl, but tall for her age, and still a little awkward in her movements. Her face was gentle, but with an eagerness in it, a holding back and a coming forward all at once. Her eyes were gray, framed in dark lashes; they often looked far off into the distance, at nothing.

She had been six when her father was killed in a Saxon raid, and her mother, daughter to an Irish King, had gone back to live in Ireland. It was thought that the young girl would be better off at Thane than among the sod huts and wooden halls of Armagh, to which Patrick had only recently brought the civilizing influence of Christianity.

She missed her father, who used to toss her in the air, and who would lift her sometimes to his saddle and ride out with her across the fields and meadows of Nairn, their home, and who smelled of peat smoke and heather. But mostly she missed her mother, who used to tell her stories about the Little People, who had been in Ireland before the Celts or even the Fenians. She dreamed that she met them, and was kind to them, and that they loved her, and came each week to drink blackberry shrub with her, or the juice of the hard little apples that grew in the orchards outside the walls.

Otherwise, her only companions were her eight-year-old cousin, Godwin, and Dame Margit, who had been her nurse and was now housekeeper at Thane.

In the schoolroom of the Keep, which looked out on the courtyard, and had once been the nursery, the Abbot of Swynneddfod was instructing his two pupils in astronomy, or the science of the heavens. The Abbot was an elderly man, on the stout side; he wore the black cowled gown of the Benedictines, and his gray hair was cut in a crown around his head. He was a learned man. He declared that the stars and planets were hung in the sky a hundred miles above the earth. "They are not illuminated during the day," he said, "because it is thought the sun gives light enough; at night they are lighted by the angels assigned to that task.

"There are one thousand seven hundred and thirty-four stars, and seven planets: the Sun, the Moon, Jupiter, Mars, Saturn, Mercury, and Venus, which is also called Trathnona Realta, the Evening Star."

"You can make a wish on it," said Penrhyd, "over your left shoulder."

"The earth," continued the Abbot, "extends from the ocean in the east which bathes the shores of Sogdiana and Ophir, to our own ocean in the west. The sun, moon, and stars rise from below earth's eastern edge, move in a circle above us, and descend into the sea a short distance beyond Ireland."

Ireland, thought Penrhyd, and trembled slightly. The vast mysteries of science, the enormous reaches of the heavens as described by Odo, the bright and beaming day, the secret night with its sudden, heart-stopping birdsong . . . the noonday fragrance of honeysuckle and sweet fern, the moon sailing the night-blue sky, drawing her heart after it like a tide . . . and Ireland, across the sea, where the sun went down, all in the green of evening and the rose of dusk . . . how strange and beautiful and frightening the world was!

Her mother lived in Ireland.

The good Odo assured his young charges that God was watching over them. "Not a sparrow falls," he declared, "but is noted in heaven." Hearing this, Godwin grew pale and hung his head, for he had that very morning brought down a young cuckoo with his slingshot. The question was —did God also watch over cuckoos? "He watches everything," said Odo; and inspired by a mystic joy, he exclaimed:

"Each of us has a guardian angel appointed by heaven."

The two young people were silent, awed by the importance of such a statement. And Penrhyd gazed at the Abbot with shining eyes. She imagined a being with immense white wings, dressed in gleaming samite; she had forgotten how many threads were interwoven in the cloth; perhaps he would be accoutered in golden armor instead. But when she tried to describe her vision to Odo, the Abbot hesitated. "Ten thousand angels," he remarked, "are said to dance upon the head of a pin. In which case, a full suit of armour . . ."

He paused, reflecting. "On the other hand," he admitted, "it is known that witches can change themselves into small animals, or even frogs; so it should be possible for an angel to dance, lightly clad, upon the head of a pin on one occasion, only to appear on another armed cap-a-pie, with sword and buckler."

"My guardian angel would never look like a frog," said Penrhyd.

"I am sure he would not," agreed the Abbot.

Below him in the courtyard Odo could hear the voices of men and women, the clang of iron, the clatter of hard-shod feet on the cobbles, the rattle of pots and pans. Looking down through the narrow, unglazed window of the schoolroom, he saw beneath him the daily bustle and business of the Keep, the sling-maker at work on his slings, two apprentices practicing at single-stick, laundresses at the water tubs, the armorer testing the heft of a spear, the farrier fitting a shoe to a horse's hind hoof, Dame Margit, the nurse and housekeeper, crossing the inner yard with her great cluster of keys swinging from her belt, and with two maids behind her with baskets of linen; Sir Anglas, the Steward, watching his men unload a cask of heather beer from a dray. And the Abbot was struck anew by the richness of life, which even in the midst of confusion and the fall of empires gave evidence of God's continuing grace.

At the same time he noted how few men-at-arms there were to be seen in the courtyard, and real-

ized with a sinking heart that Morven had taken
most of the fighting men with him when he had
gone to join Arthur. It occurred to him that the
Keep was poorly defended in case of disaster.

If Thane were lost, the Monastery at Swynneddfod would be in flames soon after. "Thy will be
done, Lord," he murmured. But unlike earlier
Christians, he did not relish the thought of martyr-
dom.

"There is a Fair at Llangford," said Penrhyd,
"with strange animals and curious beasts and jug-
glers. And there are booths for fairings, and magicians."

The Abbot roused himself with difficulty from
his reflections. "Those are heathen things," he said.
"Omnes immundi spiritus . . ."

Penrhyd sighed, and her eyes took on a dreamy
look. "I should dearly love to see a curious beast,"
she said. "A wyvern, or a unicorn."

"God forbid," said the Abbot.

"The Saxons have horns growing out of their
head," said Godwin. "Margit told me."

"Dame Margit," Odo admonished him.

"Yes, sir," Godwin agreed. "She said they come

to a castle, and they knock it down. Then they reap the women."

He hesitated a moment. "I think that's what she said," he added uncertainly.

Penrhyd had turned pale; she remembered the burning of Nairn, and exclaimed fearfully,

"Surely they will not come to Thane itself?"

Odo took a deep breath, and replied with assurance: "They would not dare to attack so strong a keep." But he was not sure that he believed it.

CHAPTER 2

A wandering harper entertained the ladies of the castle that night. Accompanying himself on a three-stringed harp made of dark bog oak, he sang of the love of Tristram and Ysot, and of Yseult of the White Hands. When he was finished, the ladies wept, and some applauded. But old Sir Anglas, the Steward, gazed moodily into his beer, and remarked to young Thomas of Glen Daur, who had come to serve Lord Morven as squire:

"I can remember when the harpers sang of battles, not of love."

"It was before my time," said Thomas. "I do not remember it."

"Nor were the ladies so delicate in those days," said Sir Anglas. Gazing at the young man over the brim of his beer jar, he demanded:

"Would you not rather ride a horse to battle than pluck a rose beneath some lady's bower?"

Thomas of Glen Daur returned a candid answer to this question. "No," he said.

Sir Anglas put his beer down on the table with a thump. "There are too few of us left who remember the old days," he said. "And of those few, too many are too old. Old men are of no use in battle; they fall early, and tangle people's legs."

He sighed heavily. "My own great-great-great-great-grandmother fought like a man," he said, "with bronze sword and scythe-wheel chariot. Like Boadicea the Queen, she kept her own stone axe within easy reach above the chimneypiece."

He fell silent, thinking how hard it was for Arthur to keep his fighting men together, and how the Princes of Britain fought each for his own advantage rather than for the whole. "When we are gone," he thought, "they will be picked off one by one like lice, and darkness will cover Britain like a night."

"Sir," said Thomas of Glen Daur, "I would be in battle now, with my Lord Morven, but that he thought me too young. But I have always heard it said that a man fights better for a woman's love."

"Na," said Sir Anglas bitterly, "they tell you that in Camelot. But no man ever fought without handicap, that wore a woman's favor into battle."

"I cannot say," replied the young man courteously, "never having fought in battle, or worn a woman's favor."

"Time enough for both," said Sir Anglas, and put his nose in his beer.

Upstairs in the nursery, Godwin and Penrhyd lay sleeping, the girl on a good mattress with a featherbed over her, the boy on a straw pallet, covered with his cloak, as was proper for a warrior. He slept on his side, twitching and tossing; but Penrhyd lay as quiet as a lily, and dreamed of angels. The moonlight, slanting in through the narrow window, touched her face; and she saw her guardian angel as she had imagined him, white as snow, and dressed in samite, which was woven of six separate threads, a fact which made her happy. "Lady," he said, "the night is dark, and there is a long way to go, and strange things on earth and in heaven." Odo stood beside her, and she said to him: "This is my guardian angel." "As to that," said Odo, "we shall see; let him dance upon a pin." At this the angel turned into a frog, and began to dance on a lily pad, and Penrhyd wept. But Godwin aimed his slingshot at the frog, who dove into the dark waters of the tarn, leaving one samite-clad arm pointing to the heavens. "He is not an angel," said Dame Margit, "but a sorcerer; he will come out of the water as a goat." However, he appeared from a grove of trees in a rosy light and with his great wings hung like two white harps behind his back. "My name," he said, "is . . ."

She woke against her will, knowing that he had not told her his name, or else that she had forgotten it. It was already day; in the cold morning light, in the great hall of the castle, which had not yet been cleared of the night's feasting, Godwin was greedily exploring the broken meats, the scraps of pastry, and the lees of the wine.

Dame Margit agreed with her that it was a very upsetting dream. "His not telling you his name," she said; "I find it very strange indeed."

"He told it to me," said Penrhyd, "but I have forgot."

"Be that as it may," said her nurse, "he had no business turning himself into a frog."

She went on to say that in her opinion he had acted more like a sorcerer than an angel. "That is what you said in my dream," cried Penrhyd in astonishment, to which Dame Margit replied that although she could not be held accountable for what she said in other people's dreams, in this case she had probably been right.

"I wish that I had learned his name," said Penrhyd, "for it is a comfort, I think, to know the name of one's guardian angel."

"At least," said Dame Margit, "you might tell me what he looked like. Was he handsome? Of commanding presence, I imagine . . . Did he remind you of anyone you know, such as your uncle, or the Abbot, or even Sir Anglas, although I cannot conceive of it."

Penrhyd's cheeks turned pink. "He did look a little like Thomas of Glen Daur," she admitted. "At least, I think he did; but not, of course, when he was a frog."

"Well," said Dame Margit, "I do not have much knowledge of dreams, but I see where Father Odo has arrived for his lesson, and perhaps he will tell us what it means."

The Abbot, who had ridden over from Swynneddfod, dismounted from his donkey and crossed the courtyard with a thoughtful expression. The news, he was obliged to admit to himself, was not good. Arthur's forces, weakened by the absence of Prince Cador's men, who had decided at the last moment to return to their homes in time for the wine-making, as well as the sudden, unlooked-for defection of Sir Modred, who had taken his entire force of knights and fighting men into Cerdic's camp in return for the promise of a kingdom, had left the armies of Britain depleted, and greatly outnumbered by the enemy who waited for them at

Salisbury Plain. With Modred's mounted knights against him, Arthur must lose the advantage of his own horse, and the Briton with his pike, his bill-hook, and his sling was no match for the Saxon with his tough bull-hide shield and his seaxe, the sharp throwing axe. "Let us hope that the Archbishop has not forgotten to say his prayers," Odo thought, having left his own Brothers on their knees at the Monastery, between Prime and Tierce.

Nevertheless, he paid attention to Penrhyd's dream, for he knew that dreams often foretold the future. Thus, for instance, Joseph was able to prophesy to Pharaoh the coming lean years, and the fat. "There are many animals mentioned in Holy Writ," he said, "including the ass, the lion, and the lamb. But nowhere is there any mention, to my knowledge, of frogs, except in the plagues with which God afflicted Egypt. Therefore, when your angel turned into a frog, one must believe the auspices to be bad; yet appearing again in a rosy light, the future might be said to appear bright. You say he emerged from a grove of trees; were they oak, perhaps?"

Penrhyd wrinkled up her nose in thought. "No," she said at last, "they were not oak."

"I am glad of that," said the Abbot, "for otherwise we might have been faced with the presence of a Druid spell. The trees of Holy Writ are the cedar, the tamarinth, or tamarisk, the pine, the olive, and the fig."

"They were none of them," said Penrhyd, who had never seen any of those mentioned except pine, and only a small stand of it at that. "But why would he not tell me his name?"

"As far as I know," said the Abbot, "the names of angels were not generally announced; I can think of only one exception to this rule, in the case of the angel Gabriel, who introduced himself by name to Zacharias, the father of the Baptist. But he was an Archangel, of a higher order. Possibly the name of your own angel would have sounded strange to you, and he therefore forbore to trouble you with it."

Seeing that the Abbot appeared weary, Dame Margit hurried off to fetch him a bowl of herb tea, and Odo sank down on a stone bench and gazed somberly before him. He had spent most of the night in prayer, and his limbs and body ached. But he had his work to do, and rousing himself after a while, he inquired of Penrhyd, who had seated herself at his feet:

"Where is your cousin Godwin?"

The boy was late for his lesson. Stuffed with the leavings of stale food and sour wine, he had taken his slingshot out to the moat's edge, meaning to aim at some ducks, and had been taken suddenly sick. Thomas of Glen Daur found him there, green as an apple, and ready to die. The young squire held him while he retched, and then laid him down on the grass beside the bank, wiped him off with a napkin, and sprinkled water on his face. "Now then, Master Godwin," he said, "you can be easy, for it has all come up, and you're as empty as a used cask." This unfortunate allusion caused Godwin to retch again, and Thomas held his head. "It was something I ate," said Godwin feebly. "And drank," said Thomas, "from the smell of it."

The child lay and rested awhile. The sun was warm on his small, cold body, and a little color crept into his face. "I think I would like a jar of cow's milk," he said presently, "but I would liefer not go through the buttery, for Dame Margit will see me with my blouse dirty."

"Stay here," said Thomas, "and I will fetch your milk for you, and warm it as well."

"You might bring me a bannock, too," said Godwin, who was feeling better.

When the squire returned with the milk and the bannock, he found young Godwin much improved in spirits, and able to sit up and to cast about for his sling, which had fallen into the bushes. "Look," said Godwin; and fitting a pebble into it, he let fly at a duck in the moat, but missed. "I am not very good at it yet," he said apologetically.

"That will come," said Thomas; "it is a fine weapon."

"Yes, it is," agreed Godwin happily; "you could kill a wyvern with it."

"I have seen a wyvern at the Fair," said Thomas, "and it is a very large animal."

As they were sitting there talking, a red doe ran out of the woods onto the cleared land on the far side of the moat, followed a moment later by a dappled fawn. "There goes in God's sight a mother and her child," said Thomas, "but it is only venison after all." He shook his head in puzzlement. "These are mysteries," he said, "like the black men who tend the unicorn at the Fair."

"Penrhyd says there are magicians at the Fair," said Godwin, "who also do mysteries."

"I do not know about that," said Thomas, "but perhaps your cousin saw something magical that I did not."

"She wasn't there," said Godwin; "it was all talk."

He was silent for a while, watching the deer across the water. "Did you really see the unicorn?" he asked at last.

"Yes," said Thomas, "and it is blacker and uglier than I thought, and lower to the ground."

"Did you ride upon it?" asked Godwin eagerly. The young squire shook his head. "It is a heavy beast," he said, "and would do better in battle than as a pleasure mount or with its head in some maiden's lap."

"Why should it put its head in a maiden's lap?" asked Godwin in surprise.

[23]

"I do not know," said Thomas, "but I have been told that is the way to tame it."

All this was highly interesting to Godwin, who had never enjoyed a conversation of such scope before. He realized that there was a great deal to learn in the world besides the dates of history and the names of the planets, and inquired curiously:

"Is my cousin a maiden?"

"I should think so, surely," said Thomas warily, "but too young yet and too angular."

"Why," said Godwin, "should maidens be otherwise?"

"I do not rightly know," said Thomas uncertainly.

"But would you wish them so?" asked Godwin.

"I cannot really say," replied the squire, "never having known any."

CHAPTER 3

Arthur was defeated at Salisbury Plain; mortally wounded, he managed to reach Avalon, and there, to the best of men's knowledge, died, for he was never seen again. Among the dead who lay heaped in windrows on the battlefield and around the fallen standard of the Dragon, were Sir Modred and Lord Morven of Thane.

When the news reached the Keep it caused general consternation, some wishing to leave at once without knowing where they were going, others preferring to stay behind the walls. At noon Sir Anglas gathered all the people into the great hall. Dressed in his battle armor, the old Steward expressed his determination to remain where he was. "I shall defend the Keep," he said.

He explained that its walls were strong, that there was a sufficient water supply, and enough grain to withstand a siege of several weeks; and went on to say that it was, in any case, their only hope. "However," he said, "those of you who prefer to take your chances in the forests or on the moors and in the marshes, may leave if you wish. Perhaps you will succeed in reaching the western mountains, or perhaps not, but in any case it will be a cruel journey."

He fell silent, gazing out across the sea of faces turned up to him, many of which were known intimately to him. "We must all die someday," he said, "when the time comes. No one lives forever, except in song. When I meet my great-great-great-great-grandmother, who fought with Boadicea, I hope it will be with a sword in my breast, and not with an arrow in my back.

"At sunup the great doors will be bolted and the bridge across the moat taken up. If you leave, you must do so at once, or during the hours of the night."

All day the Keep was like a beehive of activity, as some prepared oil and pitch to be heated for the defense, counted the sacks of grain, and sharpened their swords on the sharpener stone in the courtyard. Dame Margit and her women stacked linen for bandages and mixed salves, drew water, and boiled herbs and simples for poultices. Only a few left the Keep, crossing the moat with many backward looks and slipping into the forest like shadows.

At sundown the Abbot arrived, somewhat out of breath, but composed and calm. "The Saxons are within a day's march of Swynneddfod," he announced, "and my monks have fled." He admitted that he had not tried to stop them. "I have seen monasteries sacked," he said, "and there is nothing edifying about it. The death of a poor

monk, or even an Abbot, does not bring the kingdom of heaven any nearer, in my opinion, for evil
goes on as it did before.

"Besides," he added, "I was charged with the
education of two young Christian souls, and it is
my duty to continue it."

"It will be quite an education," said Sir Anglas
grimly, "when the Saxons bring their storming
ladders to the walls."

"To be frank," said Odo, "I do not expect to be
here to see it. I intend to take Master Godwin and
Lady Penrhyd to the Priory at Malmesbury."

"That will be no easy journey," said Sir Anglas.

Odo agreed that it would not be easy. "But
once they are there," he said, "they will be safe,
at least for a time; and meanwhile you will not
have them on your mind."

"That is true," Sir Anglas admitted; "for they
will be in God's care. But it would be wrong for
a young gentlewoman to journey through the
countryside without a female attendant, and with
only an Abbot and a boy of eight for company."

"Let me have Dame Margit then," said the Abbot, "that was Penrhyd's nurse."

"Gladly," said Sir Anglas, "but tell her to leave her keys behind her."

When it was known that Penrhyd, Godwin, and Dame Margit were to leave the Keep, many came to bid them good-by, to ask them to bear messages to kinfolk, and to urge them to beware of the night damp. "And watch out for basilisks," said the farrier, "for they bewitch horses, causing them to cast their shoes."

The young squire, Thomas of Glen Daur, went to look for Sir Anglas, and finding him at evening prayers, waited outside the chapel until they were done. Then, when the Steward came out at last, dusting off his knees, he stepped forward and begged permission to accompany the Abbot and his charges on their journey. "Sir," he said earnestly, "they need someone to guard them in the forest."

Sir Anglas looked at him, and his lip curled. "You?" he asked. "The plucker of roses?"

Thomas flushed, but met his gaze squarely. "I know the forest paths," he said, "and what mosses are safe to eat."

The old Steward sighed heavily. "I cannot spare

a fighting man," he said. "Perhaps I have no choice. Do you have a sword?"

"No," said Thomas. "But I have my knife."

"What good would that be," asked Sir Anglas, "against a Saxon axe?"

"None at all," said Thomas cheerfully; "but neither would a sword, without a buckler and armored hat. And if I were dressed in chain mail, I should not get very far without a horse, and I do not have a horse.

"A knife," he added, "is very handy for peeling turnips, and for small animals."

The ghost of a smile played for a moment across Sir Anglas's tired face. "You have a light heart," he said. "Perhaps it will serve you where heavier metal might fail." And placing his hand for a moment on Thomas's shoulder, he added:

"Go, then; and God be with you."

He turned away. "I do not really have a light heart," said Thomas, but Sir Anglas was already out of earshot.

By sundown Penrhyd and Dame Margit were ready, having packed a woolen blanket, a feather-

bed, and a cooking pot, as well as a square of per-
fumed soap, a little leather box, empty, a bay-
berry candle, a packet of ribbons for Penrhyd's
hair, a jar of honey, a cold joint, a bronze hand
mirror, a dozen barley cakes or bannocks, a piece
of tapestry in work for the long evenings, a mid-
dling crock of butter, and a pair of warm drawers,
for the journey.

They found Master Godwin hiding under
Penrhyd's bed, clutching his slingshot. "I thought
I saw a mouse," he said when they dragged him
out by the heels, his face streaked with tears. "He
went into a little hole.

"I'm going to kill him," he cried, struggling for-
lornly in Dame Margit's arms. "Rotten old mouse!"

Dame Margit wept into her handkerchief. "They
killed his father," she said. Many of the other
women wept too, but Penrhyd did not. She went
about her packing with dry eyes and with a
strange, distant look on her face. It was too much
like something that had happened before, it was
like a bad dream dreamed for the second time:
her mother and herself fleeing from their home as

she was fleeing now. Was Ireland waiting for her, too? And would she someday marry an Irish King?

Descending to the buttery, she took down a heavy silver goblet, to pack into her featherbed along with her own little porridge bowl. "At least," she said, "I will not come without a bride's gift."

In the wavering shadows and faint puddles of light cast by the pine-knot torches in the courtyard, Odo and his companions took leave of Sir Anglas. Odo pressed his hand, and Dame Margit kissed him on the mouth. "For the first time," she said, "and the last."

"Thank you," he said. "If we meet in heaven I shall remember that."

Then the great doors of the Keep were opened and the little band clattered across the bridge and into the darkness of the trees, the Abbot on his donkey, carrying the featherbed, Dame Margit upon a jennet with Godwin up behind, Penrhyd on her own moorland pony, and Thomas of Glen Daur walking by her side.

It was dark and silent in the forest, and Godwin clung tightly to Dame Margit's ample waist. They followed along the path, keeping as close as possible to the Abbot's donkey, which seemed able to pick its way among the trees.

"Are you afraid?" asked Thomas, with his hand on Penrhyd's stirrup.

"No," she said, "only of this silence which makes my ears prickle."

"There are many miles of darkness," said Thomas, "between here and Malmesbury."

"That is no help to me," said Penrhyd, "for as it is, I can barely see my pony's head in front of me."

"I will hold your foot," said Thomas, "for comfort."

"If you wish," said Penrhyd.

"Is that not better?" asked Thomas presently.

"It is very comforting," said Penrhyd.

Up ahead in the darkness the Abbot of Swynneddfod, clasping the featherbed in which were packed the ladies' belongings, peered anxiously around him, listening to the stillness of the night. He could see nothing; and except for the creak of leather and the occasional snapping of a twig, he heard not a sound. "All of Britain lies in darkness," he thought; "meadow, field, moor, and forest, with only here and there a tiny hamlet glowing like a spark in a marsh. Yet each cottage light is a beacon, beckoning to the angelic choirs, who are forever singing a Te Deum to the Lord, but also, alas, signaling to the demonic hordes who feed upon men's souls as well as their bodies, and who haunt the earth in the form of serpents, goats, dragons, owls, wolves, and ravens, and women with pointed ears, and a tail."

Alarmed by his own thoughts, he crossed himself and also made the old Celtic Sign of the Horns, for the forest in its very stillness seemed full of evil things, and it might be that the angelic choirs were not paying attention. "Let the old gods keep their hands off me," he said, "seeing that we are Christians; and may the witches stay in their holes as we pass through, and the light of Holy Church illumine our path, while keeping us hid from the Saxons and the Jutes."

It was cold in the forest, and Godwin moved more closely to Dame Margit's warmth to keep himself from shivering. The movement of the jennet was making his stomach heave. "Do you think there are Saxons in the forest?" he whispered, to which Dame Margit replied in a low voice that there were worse things, such as bears, wolves, and basilisks.

"I am going to be sick," said Godwin, and slid from his seat to the ground. At once Dame Margit halted her beast, causing the pony, which had been following close behind, to bump into it. The pony shied, Thomas let go of Penrhyd's ankle, and Penrhyd, losing her stirrups, went over her mount's head in a slow descending arc. "Now you've done it!" she said to no one in particular as she hit the ground.

Almost at once a pair of strong arms lifted her up, and a deep voice said in her ear:

"Lady, the night is dark, and there is a long way to go, and strange things on earth and in heaven."

Penrhyd's mouth fell open, and she stared up in amazement at the tall figure whose face she could not see. "I have heard those words before," she said, "in a dream. Was it you who said them to me?"

"Yes," said the figure; "it must have been."

At that moment Thomas came hurrying back, his hand on his dagger. "Who are you?" he cried.

"And what are you doing?" But Penrhyd placed herself in front of the stranger, with outspread arms. "He is my guardian angel," she said; "and his name is . . ."

She hesitated, looking questioningly up at the darkness which covered the stranger's face. "My name is Azael," he said.

CHAPTER 4

After that, for the remainder of the night, Azael
and Thomas of Glen Daur walked on either side
of Penrhyd, each holding her by the foot. Thomas
was not pleased with the arrangement, but he saw
no way of protesting without appearing to be
selfish, and he was, besides, somewhat awed by the
great figure of the stranger, whose features he was
unable to make out because of the darkness of the
night and because they were hidden in some sort of

cowl or shawl. He was not so much surprised to be in the company of an angel—if he was an angel—as he was vexed at himself for having allowed Penrhyd to fall off her pony. It was not a very good beginning.

Meanwhile the others had gone on ahead and it was some time before Penrhyd and her two companions caught up with them. They found the Abbot with Dame Margit and Godwin in an open glade over which the night sky with its quiet stars cast a faint glow, no more than a suggestion of light, a shade less of darkness. "Margit dear," said Penrhyd, "do you remember my dream? Here is my guardian angel, who plucked me from the ground where I had fallen."

And to the Abbot, she said:

"Reverend Father, this is Azael."

"Ah, then he has told you his name," cried Dame Margit, and attempted to get down to make the angel a curtsy, but was restrained by Godwin's tight hold on her waist.

Odo, however, stood his ground. "Azael," he said suspiciously; "what sort of a Christian name is that?"

The angel seemed to smile in the darkness, but they could not see his face, which seemed even blacker than the night. "It is not a Christian name at all," he said. His voice was deep and pleasing, but slightly guttural.

"Are you a demon?" cried Odo; and seizing his Crucifix, held it out in front of him. "In the name of Our Blessed Lord and Savior," he exclaimed, "begone from here!"

"You are mistaken," said Azael gently; "I, too, am a creature of God, and love and worship the Prince of Peace. But I go far back in time; I am not even sure how far. When I was created, Adam was still only a longing in God's mind."

And he added simply:

"I have only been Christian for a little while."

"Well," said the Abbot grudgingly, "I shall have to think about that."

"At least," said Dame Margit, "he has not turned into a frog."

"I do not think it matters very much if his name is Christian or not," said Penrhyd, "with the Saxon war host so close behind."

"The child is right," said Azael, "although I am

sure that they are not as near as you think; and since you must all be weary, I suggest that you take this opportunity to rest awhile in this glade, to snatch a few hours of sleep while you can."

"And who will stand watch while we sleep?" asked Thomas sensibly. "I will," said Azael. "I will watch with you then," said Thomas, suppressing a yawn.

The Abbot thought it an excellent suggestion, and climbing down from their animals, the companions tethered them to the bushes, and unpacking the featherbed and the blanket, laid them out on the ground and were soon asleep, the Abbot, having recited his Lauds, at one side of the bed, with Penrhyd and Dame Margit next to him and Godwin between them for warmth.

Thomas seated himself upon a stone and began to sharpen his knife, meanwhile keeping one eye on the surrounding forest and the other on Azael, who stood quietly within the shadows of some alders at the edge of the clearing. But little by little the young squire's eyes grew heavy, his head drooped, and with a sigh he, too, presently fell asleep, and tumbled from his rock to the soft

ground. Azael gently covered him with his own
cloak against the dew, and resumed his watch.

The stars wheeled slowly across the heavens,
the Great Bear sank out of sight, and the small,
late moon rose in the east, touching the faces of
the sleepers with its milky light. All was silent;
even the animals slept; and Azael felt the peace of
God flood his being. To be a part of such beauty,
of the star-spun heavens, the slow-moving wind
sweet with the scents of the forest, the quiet,
dreaming earth hushed in the waiting night, filled
him with joy as always. Far in the depths of the
forest, a wolf howled; its call was answered by another, and presently the entire pack burst into
song, savage, mournful, and musical. "Even in
the wilderness," thought Azael, "there are those
who hunger for more than food."

A small brown bear lumbered across the glade
in the moonlight, causing the pony and the two
donkeys to strain anxiously against their tethers.
Seeing the angel, it stopped, raised itself upon its
haunches, and appeared to make a clumsy obei-
sance. Azael blessed it, and with a snuffling sigh it
dropped to all fours again and went on its way.

Azael's love went out to the bear, and to the sleeping girl. He was lonely for human warmth; it had always been that way with him, whether in the desert or in the city, among the hermits of the Thebaid, or in the palaces of Rome, under the frowning fortresses of the Goths, or in the oak and beech forests of Britain. Even earlier, he remembered the Wilderness of Sin, although he had not been on duty then, and the wars of the Jews; and before that, the Cities of the Plain, the fire on Sodom, and the waters that covered the earth. But always he had been drawn to man, feeling his bewilderment, pitying his grief, wondering at his passion, and listening to his prayers.

The small, curved horn of the waning moon rose higher in the sky, sailing westward over the forests and the moors toward Malmesbury and beyond, lighting the tops of the Welsh mountains and the waves of the Irish Sea. The mist began to rise in the glade like breath in a frosty night, intensifying the odor of damp forest earth and leaf mold, fungus, and the small forest flowers. "Lord," said Azael reverently, "You have made all things beautiful, each in its season and place. Boruchu es Adoshem."

The mist crept higher, curling over the sleeping forms and shrouding the trees. In the gray foggy light of early dawn the Abbot woke, crept out from under the featherbed, and said his prayers. Then, rising from his knees, he gazed about him uncertainly. "Are you there, Thomas?" he called.

He was answered by a low snore. But Azael spoke from the thicket of hazel trees. "I am here, Abbot."

"I cannot see you," said the Abbot, peering in his direction. "The fog is too thick. Have you been here, then, all night?"

"I have been keeping watch," said Azael.

"And you heard nothing?"

"Nothing. Only the birds of the night."

"No horns in the forest?"

"None."

"Well," said the Abbot, "that's good." He yawned, and stretched himself. "I think," he said, "that I will cut a few slices from the cold joint, to break our fast; and with the bannock cakes, and a little honey, and some water from the spring . . ."

He checked himself, and groaned. "What spring?" he exclaimed. "I do not remember there being a spring . . ."

"There is a spring," said Azael, "of clear water, a few steps inside these trees. If you will hand me a jug, or jar, I will fill it, and fetch it back to you."

"I can find only a cooking pot," said the Abbot unhappily.

"That will do very well," said Azael.

By the time he returned with the water, the Abbot had already cut himself a dollop of meat from the cold roast, and having said his grace, was briskly munching on a bannock. The sleepers still lay without moving, except that Godwin was beginning to twitch.

The mist was still too heavy and the light too dim for the Abbot to see more of Azael than the tops of his legs as he stood before him. "I would offer you a bannock," the Abbot said, "but if you are, as you say, an angel, you would refuse it."

"Why?" asked Azael.

"You cannot be corporeal and incorporeal at

the same time," said the Abbot; "you cannot be spirit and with a body's appetites."

"Can I not?" Azael remarked, and leaning down, took the bannock from Odo's hand and bit into it. "It is very good," he said.

Godwin awoke, and went off to make water. "Not that way," said Odo; "that is the direction of the spring." The sky to the east was faintly green now, and the mist began rising off the ground into the air. Thomas stirred under Azael's cloak, and Dame Margit sat up, shivering, her head in her hands. But Penrhyd still nestled under the feather-bed; in her sleep her face was that of a child, peaceful and secret. "We had best waken her," said the Abbot, dusting the crumbs from his mouth and wiping his hands on the ground, "and the young squire too, for we must be on our way before too long."

"Arthur is slain," said Dame Margit despondently, "and with him Morven of Thane and the Lords of the Cymri, and I do not know where we are going, or why."

"You will feel better with something inside you," said the Abbot, offering her a bannock.

"I will fetch another pot of water," said Azael, "for the ladies to freshen their faces." His back was to them as he spoke. He bent, picked up the pot, and walked off in the direction of the spring.

Thomas of Glen Daur arose, knuckling the sleep from his eyes. There was a flush of yellow light by now above the treetops, and the mist had risen clear off the ground; in the open space of the glade the first pale blue showed in the sky. The air was fresh and cold; it gave promise of being a fine day.

They were all awake except Penrhyd when Azael returned from the spring. The light was on his face as he came out of the woods, and they sat suddenly arrested, silent, too amazed to speak. He went over to the featherbed where Penrhyd still lay sleeping, and stirred it gently with his foot. "Come, lady," he said; "waken. It is time to be up."

She turned and stretched under the coverlet, pink and warm and yawning like a kitten. She opened her eyes and looked up at him; and her eyes stayed open, gray as the heather and round as saucers. "Why," she stammered; "why . . ."

The being who gazed down at her was not as she remembered, nor was he clothed in white samite. His face was darker than the heart of a tarn. "Why," she cried, "your skin is black!

"You are a black man!"

"So?" said Azael simply.

CHAPTER 5

"I cannot understand," said the Abbot as they rode on through the forest, Odo on his donkey as before, and Azael striding at his side, holding on to the donkey's tail, "why God should have played such a trick on us."

"I assure you," said Azael serenely, "that He did not do so."

"But how can you be an angel," demanded Odo, "and black?"

"Why not?" asked Azael simply.

Pointing to the trees around them in which were to be seen all the colors and shades of green and yellow, the brown of the earth under their feet, the blue of the sky glimpsed occasionally above their heads, and the golden motes of sunlight dancing among the leaves, he declared:

"Colors are God's delight. He made the dark and the light, the night and the day; He made the green of the sea and of the evening sky, the blue of the lake and of the distant hills, the white of the moon daisy, the lavender of dusk. He made the heather and the gorse, the rose and the wild strawberry, the grass and the broom. He made light people and dark people, the people of the desert and of the watered plains, the people of the Horse, of the Sun, and of the Hollow Hills. All are equally dear to Him, once they have acknowledged His Kingdom."

"That may be," said the Abbot obstinately, "but there will never be such a thing as a Pict turned Christian, or a Saxon either."

"Oh," said Azael; "why so? I should have thought the Emperor of Rome a less likely prospect myself. But then, you never saw the Imperial

City, the greatest in the world, with its marble courts and palaces, its triumphant arches, its temples and its theaters, and the great Colosseum, in which so many of the early Christians were martyred. Yet, under Constantine, all Rome turned Christian, by Imperial decree. This is probably a greater wonder than that some should be white, and others black."

And when the Abbot did not at once reply, he asked gently:

"Would you have preferred me to be another color?"

"I do not know," said Odo uncomfortably. "I should have to think about it."

Behind them, on her jennet, Dame Margit said over her shoulder to Godwin, who was mounted behind:

"I am convinced this is meant to be a punishment for your having shot the cuckoo."

Godwin trembled, but something told him that such a punishment was unjust. "Then why," he demanded, "is he come to watch over Penny, and not me?"

"It is probably a mistake," said Dame Margit;

"an error in bookkeeping, such as we used to have at the Keep before I was housekeeper for your father."

"I wonder if my father killed many Saxons before he died," said Godwin.

"However many he killed," Dame Margit replied, "there are plenty more behind us.

"It is all the fault of that Gwenifer," she burst out presently, "with her bold, wanton ways."

And turning her face resolutely to the front, she remarked:

"Queen or no queen, let that be a lesson to you."

"Yes, ma'am," said Godwin meekly. "But I still don't see why Penrhyd got the angel and not me."

"Would you want a black?" demanded Dame Margit. "That is," she added, "if he is an angel, and not a wizard."

"I wouldn't care what color he was," said Godwin, "so long as he was mine."

"I must admit," said Thomas of Glen Daur, walking beside Penrhyd's pony as they followed the others along the forest path, "I was surprised to see anyone so dark-complexioned, though I have seen black men before, at the Fair."

"Maybe they were angels also," said Penrhyd.

"They had charge of the animals," said Thomas.

"Oh," said Penrhyd.

A little later she remarked:

"Where did they come from, the black men at the Fair?"

"I do not know," said Thomas. "From another country, I think."

Penrhyd nodded. "Odo has told us of countries across the sea," she said. " '*Omnis Gallia in tres partes divisa est.*' Did you know that?"

"Every child knows that," said Thomas.

She rode along for a while without speaking, breathing the cool forest air. "Perhaps in their country all the angels are black," she said at last. "Or perhaps . . ."

She hesitated a moment. "Perhaps there is some special virtue in the color," she said uncertainly.

The young squire shrugged his shoulders. "I find no virtue in it," he said. "If it were me . . ."

"Yes?" she asked.

"Why," he said, "I would choose a prettier color for you."

"Oh," she said, and blushed. "I am not very

pretty," she said, and waited for his answer.

"Perhaps not," he agreed; "but you do well enough."

It was not very much of a compliment, she thought, but she tried to feel happy about it. On the other hand, there seemed to be no point in pursuing the subject further. "Tell me about the Fair," she said. "Was it very strange and merry?"

"There was a beast there larger than a bothy," said Thomas, "having a tail both in front and behind. And the unicorn that I told your cousin Godwin about, which is a marvelous big animal, very fierce in its aspect; and tests of strength and skill, and many small booths for games of chance such as knucklebones and the like, and others to display glass beads and trinkets."

"And were there fortune-tellers, too?" asked Penrhyd.

"There were dancing women of Barbary," said Thomas, "with gold hoops in their ears."

"Oh," said Penrhyd.

"They wear bracelets on their ankles," said Thomas, "and wide skirts, and flowers in their hair."

"I do not think I will have my fortune told after all," said Penrhyd.

"I suppose," she said presently, "they walk about everywhere as they please?"

"If you mean the Barbary women," said Thomas, "they dance in front of the booths to attract customers."

"I see," said Penrhyd. "That must be very interesting."

"Why, yes," said Thomas, "it is generally thought so."

"I suppose they do a reel or a fling," said Penrhyd, "or possibly an Irish jig?"

"They do a Carthaginian dance," said Thomas; "or that is what I was told."

"I suppose they are very young and pretty," said Penrhyd.

"I think they are what is called handsome," said Thomas uncertainly.

They rode on in silence for a time. "I do not think I should like it at the Fair," Penrhyd said after a while. "It does not sound so interesting after all."

"You seem to have changed your mind very suddenly," said Thomas.

"It is on account of the animals," said Penrhyd. "I think they would frighten me."

"They are in cages," said Thomas; "and, anyway, I would stand in front of you."

"Of course," said Penrhyd, "in that case . . ."

"Besides," said Thomas, "I promised Sir Anglas."

"I see," said Penrhyd. "That was very kind of you, I'm sure. I did not know it was for Sir Anglas's sake."

He stepped forward to hold back a branch from brushing her cheek; and as he did so, caught sight of the Abbot and Azael on the path ahead. "Anyway," he said, "you do not need me any more."

"How can you say that," she cried, "when you know it is not true?"

And as he did not reply, she added: "Are you angry because I have a guardian angel?"

He kicked at a tree root. "Why should I be?" he asked coolly.

"I cannot imagine," said Penrhyd in a small voice, and sat up straighter on her pony.

As the day waned, the trees thinned out around them, and the land rose upward to the downs, which lay like a windy sea under the westering sun, with a mist of heather in the hollows, gray rock and bracken on the slopes, and the yellow of the broom. Here they came upon the old Roman road from Devizes, and followed it for a while, passing a great stone cromlech on a hill, in front of which Odo made the Sign of the Cross, while Azael went by without paying attention. "We have just passed," said Odo, "a shrine or temple of the old pagan gods, Lud, or perhaps the Corn God, or Tyr, or Ruanh of the Dark Hair.

"Do not dignify them by noticing them," said Azael; "for to do so is to accord them a significance they do not possess."

"You are right," said Odo, "but it does no harm to be sure."

"I think we are too easily seen on these bare downs," said Azael, "and we would do better to enter the forest again at the further side."

"Indeed, we would be easy pickings," the Abbot

agreed, as he turned his donkey toward the trees.

The light was beginning to fade once more, and the blue shadows came out of the forest to meet them. "I must say," remarked Dame Margit, "I would give a great deal for a roof over my head, and a soft place to lie, for I think another night on the ground would be the death of me."

"By this time," said the Abbot sternly, "many of those we left behind us are already dead," a remark which caused Dame Margit to burst into tears.

"I shall fall off," said Godwin, "if you do not stop shaking."

A short way inside the forest they began to smell the bitter odor of charred wood and broken clay, and a little farther on came to a clearing in which they could see the remains of a small farmstead, with its cattle byres, sheep pens, and beeskeps all blackened by fire. The roof still stood on the main house, but one wall had been broken through, and left black and gaping to the sky. A few farm implements lay scattered on the ground, along with a woman's kerchief and petticoat; otherwise there was no sign of life anywhere.

"The Saxons have been here before us," said Odo.

"Then we can spend the night safely," said Azael, "for they will not return for a while."

They set about making themselves as comfortable as they could. Dame Margit brought in fresh rushes for the floor to take the place of those muddied by Saxon war boots, and Thomas brought in dried bracken and a few wild apple branches to make a fire on the open hearth. Odo went in search of water; and Godwin took his sling, and looked around.

In the burned-out byre, Azael found the remains of a charred and roasted cow. Two buzzards rose heavily from the carcass as he approached, and a lynx moved back and sat down a little way off, licking its paws, and casting modest looks at the angel, who stood awhile sniffing the odor of roasted meat. "It is like the air over Canaan," he thought.

When he got back to the hut, the fire was going, and Dame Margit was brewing a pot of herb tea in the iron cauldron. Penrhyd sat before the fire, holding a battered wooden doll which she had found tossed in the bed corner; from the look on her face, she had wept a few tears for the lost child to whom it had belonged.

A little while later Godwin returned, having found a bedraggled old woman hiding behind a pile of brush at the clearing's edge. She was exhausted, and in a pitiful state, having been in the woods picking berries when the Saxons came, and having seen them set fire to the farm, kill her son, and carry off his wife and daughter. Afraid that they might return, and in terror of wild animals, she had cowered in the brush pile for two days, without food or sleep, shaking with cold at night, and mumbling her prayers.

When Odo asked her what had happened to her son's body, she replied that a great wolf had dragged it off into the forest. "It was a werewolf," she declared, "for I heard it say grace before meat, in the old language."

Breathing in the fragrance of the tea boiling in the iron pot, she added:

"I am a Christian myself."

"In that case, God's presence in this house," said Odo.

After the old woman had been given a jar of the hot, bitter tea, and a bannock, with a bite of cheese, her spirits revived, and she inquired of Dame Margit what the sleeping arrangements were. "My place has always been before the hearth," she said. And she went on to declare that they were welcome to share her son's roof, all except Azael, who must sleep outside.

"But he is an angel!" exclaimed Dame Margit in embarrassment.

"It makes no difference," said the old woman who had seen her home destroyed, and her son murdered, and had herself escaped extinction by a hairsbreadth; "I will only sleep with people of my own color."

Azael wrapped himself in his cloak and went outside and leaned against a tree. Darkness was coming on, and the chill of evening touched his face darker than the shadow in which he stood. Little by little the fire on the hearth inside the hut died down, the featherbed was laid on the floor, and the old woman got into it, elbowing Penrhyd to one side. "Now then," she said, "don't thresh about in your sleep or I shall get no rest at all."

The Abbot knelt for a long while over his evening devotions, before letting himself down onto the rushes in the bed corner where Thomas already lay asleep and snoring gently. But Penrhyd crept out to join Azael, carrying the wooden doll in her arms. "If you don't mind," she said. "I would rather sleep out here with you."

As he had done with Thomas the night before, Azael covered her with his cloak. "Have you said your prayers?" he asked; and when she shook her head, he ordered her to say an Our Father.

"Where is heaven?" she asked sleepily, when she had finished.

"It is above the earth," he said, "and below the stars."

She fell asleep, thinking for a moment, before the darkness engulfed her, that she saw enormous wings folding around him, whiter than moonlight and shadowy as the wind. But even as she watched, they turned all the bright colors of the rainbow.

CHAPTER 6

They offered to take the old woman along with them when they left the next morning, but she elected to stay where she was. "After all," she said, sitting bedraggled in the ruins of her empty hut, "I never saw you before; how do I know that you will not rob me of all I possess?"

"You no longer possess very much," said Odo kindly, "but for your information, this young lad is the son of Lord Morven of Thane, and I am the

Abbot of Swynneddfod. And Azael, as Dame Margit has informed you, is an Angel of the Lord."

"Then I don't know what you're doing around here," said the old woman decidedly, "and the sooner you're gone, the better."

As they went on through the forest in the cool morning air, Odo continued to teach his pupils the history of the world.

"The earth," he said, "is exactly four thousand five hundred and forty-three years old. The date of the Flood, which destroyed all living creatures except those in the Ark, was 1656 in the Year of the World; and Abraham entered Canaan for the first time in 2083. God said 'Abraham,' and Abraham said 'Here I am.' "

He continued:

"Jericho fell to the sound of trumpets in the year 2553, and Queen Boadicea died sixty-one years after the Death and Resurrection of Our Lord in Jerusalem."

But he noticed that Azael looked thoughtful. "Does something trouble you?" he asked gently.

"Is the earth indeed only four thousand years old, or a little more?" asked the angel. "I thought it older than that; or else the time has seemed longer."

"The dates are those worked out by the philosophers," the Abbot replied, "on the basis of ancient writings, including the first Book of the Creation. I am surprised that you, of all people, should be ignorant of history."

"The truth is," said Azael, "I know no more about what is going on than you do."

He continued simply:

"An angel is not gifted with divine knowledge; it was in the pursuit of such knowledge that Lucifer incurred God's wrath and was cast down from heaven by his fellow Archangel, Michael, who was obeying God's commands. It is true that I have lived a long time, and have seen history being made; but I had no foreknowledge of what was to take place, and was often as surprised as those involved in it. This should not seem strange to you; for you must admit that a host of angels all endowed with second sight would confuse things here on earth beyond any possibility of order."

Odo nodded his head in agreement. "I can understand," he said, "that only God can be all-knowing and all-seeing, having both the past and the future in view. But tell me," he said, suddenly grave, "why, in that case, did he pick Abraham, out of all people; or, knowing what lay ahead for His Beloved Son, why choose the Jews for His own?"

"I have often asked myself that question," said Azael sadly, "and the only answer I have been able to arrive at is that the Jews were a literary people, and had a language at once lofty and forceful. Do not forget that in the Beginning was the Word."

"I always thought that had a Gnostic sound," said the Abbot, "in addition to being fairly incomprehensible."

"My dear Abbot," said Azael, "or if you will allow it, my dear friend, the sun rises, sinks, and sets, and somehow makes its way beneath the earth to rise again. Is that comprehensible? The stars shine in the sky, yet they lie as far from heaven, which is above us, as from the earth under our feet. Giants and dragons flourished in the past, for I have seen them myself, knowing, at the time, no more of natural science than they did. As men increased in understanding, so did the heavenly host; Pythagoras, Euclid, Ptolemy, and Aristotle shared, without being aware of it, their knowledge with the angels. We were present at all the great battles of history; as interested observers we watched the siege of Troy, the wars of the Greeks, the triumphs of Alexander, and the rise of Rome, but the battles in which we ourselves took part, or in which our sympathies were engaged, all took place in the Wilderness of Sin, the deserts of Sinai, among the hills of Ammon and Moab, or in the valleys of Philistia, washed by the sea air. In the thirty-third year of Our Lord, Tiberius being Emperor, and Pontius Pilate governor of Judea, our orders took us to Rome, where we became familiar with the Colosseum and the catacombs.

"It is all a mystery, no more to mortal men than to ourselves, who, obeying the commands of the Most High, must dwell among men and be responsible for them."

"Shall we ever comprehend that mystery?" asked Odo sadly.

"It is incomprehensible," said Azael; "but you will comprehend it. For men, yearning, obstinate, willful, and lonely, will continue to seek answers where angels fear to tread. What is more, I believe that God wishes you to find Him, despite all.

"And when you do," he concluded, "we who stand forever before the Throne, will know for the first time what it is that we glorify."

Seated on the bank of a small stream, they shared what was left of their provision, washing it down with the cold water which sang and tumbled among the stones. Godwin and the Abbot discussed the possibility of catching a trout for their supper, using Dame Margit's snood as a net, no one having thought to bring fishing lines; and Penrhyd, seeing some harebells growing beside a thicket across the way from them, expressed the wish to have some flowers to place in her hair, at which Thomas at once stepped into the water and started across. But when he was in the middle of the stream, his foot slipped on a rock, and he fell in, which evoked a muffled scream from Penrhyd, and from Godwin the observation that if there had been any fish in the stream before, they were certainly not there now.

Rosy with embarrassment, the young squire had just risen dripping to his feet when the thicket on the opposite bank parted and a large boar stepped out of the bushes, and started toward the stream, only to stop at sight of Thomas, his ugly snout twitching up and down to catch his scent. "Don't move!" cried Odo. "Stay perfectly still." But it was too late. Thomas was already floundering backward through the shallows, slipping and sliding, and tugging vainly at the dagger caught in his belt. "Yoicks!" cried Godwin happily, reaching for his sling; but Azael laid a restraining hand on his arm. "You will only succeed in vexing the animal," he said, and added calmly:

"You are too small to be a David, and he is not Goliath."

"Perhaps," said Odo faintly, "if we could remember the exhortation to the Gadarene swine . . ."

Azael gazed at him in surprise. "The situation does not lend itself to exhortation," he declared.

"We are not dealing here with unclean spirits."

And addressing the boar, he explained that they were a party of Christians in flight from the Saxon war host, that they meant no harm to him, and that they would be glad of his company through the forest, if he were minded to accompany them. "Thus," Azael said, "the Blessed St. Marcarius the Younger enjoyed the friendship of many wild animals, in particular that of a female hyena whose cub, being born blind, the saint was able to restore to sight. The next day the hyena returned bringing with her a magnificent sheepskin as a gift. St. Blaise also had many friends among the wolves and the bears, who used to sit in silence watching him at his prayers. And St. Mary of Egypt had her grave dug for her by a lion."

The boar stood irresolute, snuffling through his nose, his great tusks gleaming. "Now I shall not have any blue flowers for my hair," said Penrhyd sadly.

At this the great animal lowered his head, and turning to the harebells, seized several of the delicate stalks in his mouth, and making his way across the stream, laid them at Penrhyd's feet. Then, with an enigmatic expression, and with a flirt of his tail, he disappeared into the lonely silence of the forest. "Well!" said Dame Margit.

Azael looked after him with regret. "Your feelings are hurt," said Odo sympathetically, "and no wonder. It is extraordinary that he should favor a simple maiden, while showing no respect for an Angel of the Lord and an Abbot of the Church." Struck by a sudden doubt, he added:

"Perhaps he did not recognize you, because of your color."

Azael allowed himself a rueful smile. "It is not as extraordinary as you think," he said.

"In any case," said Thomas, "he was a savage animal. You did not see his little red eyes gleaming and his tusks dripping saliva, as I did, being closest to him, and halfway across the stream with treacherous footing beneath me, else I should certainly have stood my ground, and gone on to pluck the flowers and brought them back, too."

"But you didn't," said Penrhyd coolly. "It was the boar brought them."

"He was in a position to do so," said Thomas stiffly.

"When I saw you," said Penrhyd, "you were quite quaking with fright."

"I was nothing of the kind!" exclaimed Thomas. "I was wet to the skin, and shivering with the cold."

Godwin agreed with him. "You were shivering," he said, "because I saw you."

Red with mortification, Thomas hesitated; then, suddenly plucking the harebells from Penrhyd's lap, he slowly tore them to pieces. "Now," he said, "I shall do what any man would do." So saying, he plunged into the stream again, reached the other side without mishap, picked a bouquet of the blooms, and brought them back to her. "Here," he said, placing them in her arms; "at least these have not been in an animal's mouth."

Penrhyd looked at them coldly. "Thank you," she said, and let them fall into the stream at her feet, whence they floated quietly away, carrying Thomas's self-esteem with them.

"What did you do that for," he asked, "when I made the trip to please you?"

"You made the trip at the wrong time, young man," said Dame Margit.

"Nevertheless," said the Abbot soothingly, "the spirit was willing, a fact which must be taken into account."

"The boar was also willing," said Penrhyd rebelliously. "He was very sweet and dear."

The young squire stared at her in amazement. "Sweet and dear" . . . ? Merciful God! And what was he, Thomas himself, then? Was he something less than an animal?

"You had no right to tear my flowers," said Penrhyd. "They were mine, they had been given me."

Thomas's face flushed a dull red; the world's injustice, in the person of a green, angular girl, had him by the throat. "Well!" he managed at last. "The next time I'm asked to do a favor for anybody . . ."

"You will have a long wait," said Penrhyd coolly, "before anybody asks you."

CHAPTER 7

That night they sheltered in a cave, striking a fire
before the entrance, the smoke of which blew in-
ward in sufficient quantity to give Dame Margit an
attack of coughing. Godwin slept without mind-
ing it, but Penrhyd lay awake a long while, upset
by something she couldn't fit a name to. It had
something to do with life being full of sadness,
and things not being what they ought . . . or
people, either. Azael sat outside, as usual, watch-

ing the night; while Thomas, with Azael's dark
cloak over him, lay before the fire, as wakeful in
the open as Penrhyd was indoors, reflecting bitterly on the world's injustice, and women's in
particular, and how a man could lose his dignity
in a single moment, by hesitating too long, or
making the wrong decision.

In the morning they breakfasted on a little water found among the rocks, a few small white
mushrooms which Azael called "manna," and the
last crumbs of the bannocks. The hazel nuts were
still too green for comfort. During the day they
twice heard Saxon war horns far off in the forest;
and once, topping a rise with a view to the north
and east, saw a column of black smoke in the sky
in the direction from which they had come. "Do
you think it is the Keep?" asked Dame Margit
fearfully, and when the Abbot replied in the af-
firmative, she wept.

As evening fell, they found themselves coming
down through the trees to the sound of the cuckoos calling, into the valley of the Parret, with the
broad meadows and tilled fields of Malmesbury
before them. The Priory stood in a copse, sur-

rounded by its orchards, sheds, bothies, and corn-
fields, a small acre in barley, and pastures for cattle and sheep. A silver bell was tolling the angelus,
spilling a thin, sweet sound into the evening air;
and the smoke of fires from the cooking place
brought a faint fragrance of apple wood to their
nostrils. "Now God be praised," said Odo, "that
has brought us out of the Wilderness and to this
holy habitation."

They were met at the Priory gate by one of the
Brothers, who looked at them suspiciously, but
presently recognizing the Abbot of Swynneddfod,
told the others to wait outside while he led Odo
to the Prior, the venerable Bedwyr. "The peace of
God upon you, Reverend Father," said Bedwyr;
"my heart delights to see you again. What brings
you so far from Swynneddfod? . . . And, apparently, from what I can see, in some haste and dis-
array."

"Alas," said Odo, "my monastery has fallen to
the Saxons, along with its protector, the Lord of
Thane, as well as his Keep and all its people, except only for myself and my two pupils, who are
of his blood, a squire, a nurse, and an angel."

The Prior's face paled slightly and took on an expression of concern. "Dear friend," he said, "and brother in Christ, we have no accommodations here for an angel."

"I doubt he would be any trouble," said Odo eagerly, "for he was the easiest of companions on the trip."

"I do not question it," said Bedwyr, "but I fear that his presence here, being of such authority, might undermine my own; there is no telling what the Brothers might do if actually face to face with a celestial visitor; it might be difficult to control their excitement."

"In the matter of authority," said Odo, speaking with some asperity, "has the Bishop himself never visited here?"

"Certainly he has," replied Bedwyr, "but that is a matter *'sub caelum et humanitas in terram,'* whereas an angel must necessarily appear to be *'divinitas supra terram in coelis.'* "

And in a solemn and melancholy tone he continued:

"I need scarcely point out to you that there is also no provision in a Priory for a damsel and her nurse." However, noticing Odo's expression of dismay, he hastened to reassure him. "There is a villa nearby," he declared, "owned by a Roman gentleman and his wife, Aurelius and Julia Vector, who would, I am sure, be only too happy to offer a refuge to the two females, and possibly the young squire and the boy as well, thereby keeping them out of mischief."

"And the angel?" demanded Odo.

"The angel too," said Bedwyr hurriedly, "for I am not unaware of the story of the two who came to visit Lot in Sodom."

"Are you implying," said Odo, "that the Priory . . . ?"

"I am not implying anything," said the Prior coldly, "but I prefer not to take any chances."

The two holy Fathers gazed at each other quietly. "Would not the owners of the villa be embarrassed," asked Odo presently, "to have an angel as a house guest?"

"Not at all," replied Bedwyr promptly, "for they are still inclined to pagan ways, worshipping household gods, pouring libations to Mithras—for Aurelius's grandfather was a Tribune of the

Ninth Legion—and lighting fires at Beltane. Your angel would be simply another experience for them."

"But that is a Celtic custom," exclaimed Odo in surprise, "to light fires at Beltane!"

The Prior of Malmesbury sighed heavily. "That is the thing about the Romans," he remarked. "They try everything."

Clapping Odo heartily on the shoulder, he turned to enter the Priory. "Come," he said: "this is the best way to settle the matter. We will send your companions to the villa of Aurelius Vector, with one of our Brothers to show them the way, while we at the Priory will attempt to make Your Holiness comfortable in a cell recently vacated by Brother Elias, who has gone to spend the remainder of his life on top of a column."

"Don't you think that I ought to accompany my pupils?" asked Odo uneasily, thinking how much better off he would be in the villa than at the Priory, but Bedwyr refused even to hear of it.

"It would cost me a thousand years in purgatory," he said, "were I to turn a Christian away from my door."

As Bedwyr had expected, Aurelius Vector and his wife welcomed the travelers with pleasure. They were a middle-aged couple, in good repair, which was more than could be said for the villa, which had begun to show signs of age and lack of care. In the atrium the plaster was peeling, and the colors of the frieze which decorated the walls had faded, and was overlaid with smoke from the braziers which warmed it in winter. Small bits of tile were missing here and there from the tessellated floors, and the once elegant side rooms had been turned into storage bins for sacks of corn and barley and smoked hams. As the Lady Julia said to Dame Margit, "It is the fault of the times, for it is well nigh impossible to get help these days."

"Don't I know it!" exclaimed Dame Margit. "At the Keep we needed a dozen in the kitchen alone, and all I ever had at any one time was eight."

"I dare say," said Aurelius, "that life at Malmesbury won't seem very exciting to you after Thane, but I hope you won't find it a total loss. There are the village festivals, and the bonfires; and we hunt a bit, naturally—we have our horses and hounds and a falcon or two; nothing extensive, of course, but . . ."

He cast a doubtful look at Penrhyd and Dame Margit, as though he hadn't seen them before. "That is," he said uncertainly, "if you ladies care for such things. . . ."

"They don't," said Godwin, "but I do."

"Yes indeed," said Aurelius, gazing at him without enthusiasm. "Of course. Some other time, perhaps."

Penrhyd and Dame Margit were put in a small chamber off the colonnade surrounding the interior court, while Godwin and Thomas were given pallets in a side room opening on the atrium, among the grain sacks; for the villa had long ago lost its elegance and was in fact a working farm. Azael was sent off to the servant quarters at the end of the garden below the terrace, among the stables and the cattle byres. "I am sure he will not mind," said Julia to Dame Margit, "for it is really quite comfortable; and in any case, I could scarcely take him into the house itself, since I do not do so with my own people."

"He is not my servant," said Penrhyd angrily,

"nor Dame Margit's either"; but Azael hushed her. "I am sure that I shall do very well wherever I am," he said, "and it will not be the first time that I have spent the night above a manger."

As a matter of fact, it made little difference to him where he lodged, since he preferred above all to watch the slow wheeling of the stars above him through the heavens, and to see in his mind's eye the night-blue spaces of the sky in which his brothers and sisters came and went like little points of fire between heaven and earth. However, having been told to go to the servant quarters, he went, and found a dimly lit chamber set aside for the household help, who greeted him with a certain restraint, all except the Greek clerk Nicias, who offered him a comfortable mat on which to rest. "For you must be tired," he said, "having come all day through the forest."

"Thank you," said Azael, letting himself down onto the mat. "God's peace to all here."

Sitting there, he was more in the light, and the others got their first good look at him. Startled, they drew back into a corner, one or two of them making the Sign of the Horns against witches and the evil eye. "Are they afraid of me?" Azael asked in surprise, and the Greek replied that it was because of the darkness of his skin, to which they were unused. "And you," asked Azael curiously, "are you not afraid?"

"A man has nothing to fear," said Nicias, "who, respecting himself, keeps the respect of the gods."

"I see that you are a philosopher," said Azael, with which Nicias agreed.

After a while the others grew more at ease with Azael and ventured to ask him several questions, such as who was his master, and where did he come from. They also wished to know whether he had seen any Saxons in the woods nearabout. "As to who my Master is," said Azael, "and where I come from, you will have to ask the Prior, or the Abbot of Swynneddfod, who would know how to talk to you, and whom you would believe, rather than me. But as for the Saxons, I can tell you that looking behind us we saw the smoke of Thane three days' journey from here, most of it through heavy forest such as would impede a war host, though not a raiding party such as the one whose traces we came upon some two nights ago."

"That would be old Granny Foster's place," said one of the men, "for she's two days' journey from here."

"But what of Arthur, Prince of Britain?" someone asked, to which Azael answered shortly that to the best of his knowledge Arthur had perished, with many of his men. "Well, then," said the fellow, who had the small, dark face of the mountain people, "there's none left but the Powys to save the country," a remark which caused the baker, who was a Cornishman, to smite his forehead and utter a loud groan. "God could save it," said Azael, "but I do not know if He will."

"If you mean Old Lud," said the mountain man, "he won't, then."

"I do not mean Old Lud," said Azael, "and wonder at your ignorance."

"What else should they be but ignorant," asked Nicias, "being unlettered men? A man cannot be other than he is, for each must live according to his nature, trusting to the gods."

"What gods are those?" asked Azael curiously, to which the Greek replied: "They are the gods of nature, of the sky, of the sea, of the green earth, of the clouds and running streams. They are our friends and our familiars, we obey their laws, and they are with us in our households and in the fields and woods. We know they are there, for we have seen them, the lightning in the cloud, the nymph in the tree, and Venus rising from the waves."

Azael drew himself up like an eagle, spreading his arms like wings on either side of his body. "There is only one God," he declared: "the Creator of the universe."

"The Creator of the universe," said Nicias, "is pure Spirit, and as such is incomprehensible to the human mind."

"He is comprehended in the heart," said Azael.

CHAPTER 8

While Azael was endeavoring to make friends of the villa's servants, the Abbot of Swynneddfod was being taken by Bedwyr on a tour of the Priory, which contained several relics of interest, including a lock of hair from the head of St. Brigid of Kildare, whom the Prior had known in his youth when she was already an old woman; a brooch made of an amethyst with an intaglio of the Imperial Seal of Maximus, last Emperor of the West; a square of cloth said to have been cut from the cloak of Dismas, the Good Thief, and a page of parchment in the handwriting of the great Jerome. "However," said the Prior, "our greatest treasure is this"; and leading Odo up a narrow, winding stair, he opened a door and ushered him into a small square chamber where Odo found an elderly monk seated before a table on which was laid a square of parchment half covered with fine Latin characters. "This is Brother Tinian," said Bedwyr, "who is writing a history of the world."

Brother Tinian did not look up from his labors. Surrounded by little trays of colors, ink made from sea urchins and galls, a platter of gold leaf, and a basket of quills, the famous scholar continued to trace with firm strokes the story of the Creation and the history of Malmesbury Priory.

This was the work on which he had been engaged for nearly forty years. And he allowed nothing to disturb him. While the war hosts of Hengest and Octa overran the countryside, he continued with admirable composure to lay his gold leaf upon the Roman capitals, illuminating each page with animals, demons, and angelic figures.

"Here," said Bedwyr proudly, "you see the past reaching toward the future as far as it is possible to imagine. Brother Tinian is not inscribing his vast fund of knowledge onto tablets of wax, which melt and scratch, or onto stone, which is unwieldy and difficult to store. These pages of history and curious facts, which will someday instruct and uplift our children's children, constitute the greatest of man's treasures here on earth, for they signify man's ability to communicate with other men and with generations yet unborn. Without this great faculty, there would have been no Holy Writ, and St. Jerome would have lived and labored in vain."

"It is encouraging," said Odo, "to catch a glimpse of immortality in the making. I dare say the work of Brother Tinian will never be exceeded in the world."

"It is impossible for communication to go farther than this," said Bedwyr, "or for the future to improve upon Brother Tinian's labors."

The elderly scribe did not allow the presence of the two Holy Fathers to distract him, but continued to paint in blue and red the head and torso of an animal, possibly a wyvern, between the lines of the letter S. However, as Odo and Bedwyr turned to go, he lifted his nose from the parchment for the first time, and remarked:

"It was at Malmesbury Priory that the Druid Merdin, seeking to escape the spells of the witch Nimue, stopped overnight, and, being confronted by a vision of St. Sebastian, retired to the Vale of Arfon, and allowed himself to be shut up in a tree.

"However," he added, "I have not yet arrived at that point in my history."

"I too have heard of Merdin," said Odo, "and that when Prince Arthur was a child, he was instructed by him in certain mysteries. It would seem that the Druid's spells were unavailing, after all."

"By the way," said Brother Tinian, "what has become of Arthur?"

"He is dead, most likely," said Odo, "or else in Avalon, and with him the last hope of Britain."

"Dear me," said Brother Tinian mildly, "I shall have something to write about, if I ever get to it."

But if Bedwyr counted on Brother Tinian to

bring glory to the Priory, it was Brother Elias who brought it the most fame. And it was to Brother Elias's column that Bedwyr now conducted the Abbot of Swynneddfod. Once part of temple destroyed by the Scots during the time of Adrian, it stood at the far end of the old Roman town long deserted and fallen into decay; green grass grew among the cobbles, and briars sprouted from the walls and colonnades. Cats roamed through the empty forecourts of the villas, pursuing mice and butterflies across the faded tiles discolored by the birds and by the weather. A few statues still stood on the terraces, stained and dispirited, missing an arm here, a leg there; and in the dried-out fountains the dust of a hundred years had settled.

It was here that Brother Elias had elected to spend the remaining years of his life, suspended like Simeon Stylites halfway between heaven and earth. Each day some monk from the Priory brought a little basket of food to the foot of the column, whence it was lifted to the top by a string; consisting of a jar of water, a bowl of kale broth, and a dry crust, it was shared by the hermit with his friends the birds, who brought him in exchange succulent grubs, berries, and seeds of grain.

On his column, exposed to the sun, the wind, and the rain, Brother Elias battled the demons who visited him mostly at night in the guise of cooks bearing fat hampers of food, or as delectable females promising him joys unknown in heaven. But his greatest temptation came from a demon dressed in fine linen, wearing a sable cloak and a great golden earl-ring on his arm above the elbow, who offered him nothing more nor less than a place in history. To this Brother Elias always replied that he would have his place in the history which Brother Tinian was writing. And he consoled himself with this reflection.

In the morning, in the bright light of day, he rejoiced in having once more escaped Satan's wiles, and inquired anxiously of the monk who brought him his food as to how Brother Tinian was getting on. "I know," he said, "that he has not come to me yet, but I have faith in the future."

Brother Elias attracted many visitors to the town, who came to view the famous stylite on his column, and to exchange bits of news from around the countryside for prophecies and meteorological observations. Thus Brother Elias discovered that the Fair which had been located further to the north was moving south to escape the Saxons, and would presently pass along the moors above Malmesbury; while farmers from the Downs learned that the weather toward the coast was clear, except for some light clouds.

When the Prior and Odo arrived at the base of the column, Brother Elias had already finished his morning devotions, and was patiently awaiting the basket containing his meal for the day. Upon receiving it at the hands of his own Prior, the holy man expressed astonishment, and gave thanks to the Lord. He then inquired how far along Brother Tinian had got in his writing. When he heard that Arthur had been slain at Salisbury Plain, he uttered a groan and hit himself on the head. "Is there to be no end to history?" he demanded; and with a heavy sigh, he added:

"There is so much going on in the world that it is easy to lose sight of one's own contribution."

Odo replied: "There can be no question of your

[91]

contribution, Brother Elias. And yet, I cannot help but wonder whether in removing yourself to the top of a marble pillar thirty feet in the air, you have gone about the Lord's business in the best way."

At this Brother Elias turned pale, and pointing a scrawny finger at the plump Abbot, exclaimed harshly: "There is no better way to glorify God than to repent of one's sins alone and in solitude, far removed from the pleasures of the world."

"I am aware of your temptations," said Odo, "and I respect and venerate the strength with which you surmount them; but I do not recognize your description of life in a monastery, which I believe is all you have seen of the world."

"The fleshpots of Babylon," cried Brother Elias, on whose lips a little froth of saliva had appeared, "were not filled with more succulent morsels than the cooking pots of Malmesbury Priory."

"That may be true at other times of the year," said Odo, "but if so, they are filled by God's grace, to furnish His children the strength to carry on His work."

"You have forgotten the story of the Prodigal,"

declared the stylite, while a light of triumph il-
lumined his face, "who fed upon husks and swill
and yet was welcomed into his father's house as
first among all his children."

"Besides," said Bedwyr pacifically, "our Brother
Elias has added greatly to the renown of the Priory, which must certainly be to God's interest and
the advantage of the Church."

"The Church," said Odo mildly, "is also a refuge to those in fear of death and a teacher to the
living, for Our Lord said: 'I am the Resurrection
and the Life,' and called the children to Him, that
He might instruct them."

"Exactly so," said Bedwyr; "and we instruct
them by precept and example. You, my dear
friend, represent the one, and Brother Elias the
other."

"I do not know what he is an example of," said
Odo uncertainly.

Bedwyr, Prior of Malmesbury Priory, plucked
nervously at his left ear. "No doubt," he remarked,
"there is something to be said on both sides. For
surely the lives of the great hermits of the Thebaid have glorified the Lord, as has that of St.

Gelasius, who took time off from his busy life as Bishop of Rome to convert Clovis, King of the Franks, and baptize three thousand of his followers."

"Do not forget Jerome," said Odo, "who had for his pupils the noblest ladies of Imperial Rome."

"The great Anthony," declared Brother Elias from his perch thirty feet in the air, "had no need for teachers, for he received instruction from heaven itself."

The Abbot of Swynneddfod returned to the Priory in a disturbed frame of mind. It seemed to him that in some strange way he had been rebuked, that his values had been questioned and his own work belittled. And he wondered if there were perhaps more terrible battlefields of the spirit than any he had imagined on earth. "Is it possible," he asked himself, "that a life of piety and prayer, of humility, of good works, is not enough in the Lord's sight? And that an Abbot is of less importance in heaven than a madman on a pillar?"

He was arrested in the midst of these reflections by the realization that in Azael he had someone with authority to answer him; and after Nones, begged leave of the Prior to absent himself from the Priory awhile in order to pay a visit to the villa.

He found the angel alone, seated somewhat disconsolately upon the stone coping of a well used to water the barnyard animals. "Our host has taken the young people out riding," Azael said after he had greeted the Abbot; "and Dame Margit and the Lady Julia are closeted in the linen room in the villa. I am very glad to see you."

And he explained that he had spent an unusually restless night in the company of Nicias, the Greek. "He is a philosopher," he declared, "and his curiosity is endless."

With a warm smile he turned to Odo, but in a moment, with an expression of concern, he remarked: "You look depressed, my friend; has anything occurred to trouble you? Or are the Saxons closer to us than we thought?"

Odo related to Azael the events of the morning, and explained the cause of his confusion. "Is it possible," he asked, "that truth can be served by such diverse means? What I mean to say is—does God take an equal delight in the hermit alone in his cave, or the solitary stylite on his pillar, as He does in the humble cenobite who obeys the rules of his order?"

Azael pondered deeply before replying. "As to the different measures of delight with which God studies His creation," he said at last, "I cannot answer you. But I know that He loves all things, some perhaps more than others; and that there is room in heaven for all kinds, for I have seen them there.

"However, this I have observed: the solitary genius also does his Father's work, which is not so much to teach by precept or example as to glorify. If his sufferings increase his ardor, God is well served; but his anguish is not counted in heaven, where pain, hunger, and grief are unknown; and where the sufferings of St. Macedonius, who spent forty-five years of his life in an open ditch, are of no more importance than those of St. Agnes, who was martyred at the age of twelve, before her life had even begun. Or, for that matter, than the blameless days of St. Hilary, who lived comfortably in Poitiers in Aquitaine."

"Then," said Odo uncertainly, "the stylite on his pillar is no closer to paradise than an Abbot?"

"He thinks he is," said Azael, "and in that lies his reward."

CHAPTER 9

Mounted on a fine palfrey from Aurelius's stables, Penrhyd rode out with Aurelius, Thomas, and Godwin along the slopes of the Malme and across the rough pasture lands bordering the woods. It was a fine day, with the small clouds sailing slowly over, and the sky all a milky blue, and the warm air sweet with wild fern and thyme. She was happy—or perhaps not, she couldn't be sure. She knew she had every right to be sorrowful, considering the death of her uncle and all her friends at the Keep; but she was young, and death was still only a word and a fear, and so much had happened, and it was hard to be sad in bright weather. She had never ridden out from Thane with such a company, it was like the Lady Gwenifer riding out from Camelot, it was quite splendid —My Lord Aurelius on his big bay, Godwin on the pony, and Thomas on Dame Margit's jennet. . . .

Thomas: she felt a sudden depression, a flattening of spirit. Something was wrong between herself and Thomas, something had risen up between them; how had it happened? A doubt, a chilling doubt: was he the brave figure she had thought him, back there in the nursery? A hero was someone who stood up to danger, sword in hand. . . .

She bit her lip, seeing him in her mind fallen into the water, wanting to laugh, and feeling ashamed of him all at the same time, and sorry for herself. The way he had carried on about Azael, as though a person had no right to have a guardian angel. What if her angel was black? It wasn't anybody's business but her own.

But she felt sad suddenly, and determined never to speak to Thomas again, unless first addressed; and all the while longing to hear him say something agreeable, like "What lovely weather we're having," or "Are you as unhappy as I am?"

And Thomas, trotting along in the rear on Dame Margit's jennet, was no less disturbed. It was the injustice of it that rankled; anyone with any sensibility would have thanked him for wading the stream to fetch her a nosegay, and been sympathetic when he fell in. Or at least have mentioned the way he faced the wild boar with nothing but his dagger, and dripping wet besides.

And then spending the night out of doors the way she had at that old woman's farm; that was not proper at all. A young woman stayed in her featherbed with her nurse until she was married, angel or no angel. "For shame," he muttered under his breath.

"Did you say something?" she asked over her shoulder.

"No," he said.

"I thought you said something," she said.

"Well," he said, "I didn't."

"I see," she said, and rode on, looking straight before her.

Godwin, on the other hand, was enjoying himself thoroughly. Armed with his sling and some smooth pebbles, he searched for partridge or hare in the gorse, admiring the sweep of the hill, the thrill of the hunt, and the fine sight of his host as Aurelius brought the big bay gelding close to Penrhyd's palfrey to hand her a sprig of clover, or catch her scarf as it was blown from her hair.

Aurelius liked young girls; they aroused a sweet emotion in his breast, compounded of wonder and delight, and a lingering sorrow. He saw Penrhyd's young, budding breasts rise and fall beneath her light linen tunic, and he imagined what it would be like to have them rise and fall for him. It did not occur to him that they rose and fell for Thomas of Glen Daur, whom he dismissed as a fellow of no consequence.

The sight of Penrhyd's bare thigh along her horse's flank caused him to catch his breath and look away in confusion. And thinking of his fifty-odd years, he heaved a sigh before looking back again.

But even as he did so, a stone whizzed past his ear and hit Penrhyd's mount in the side. Godwin, having sighted a hare, had let go with his sling, and had as usual missed his target.

Away went the palfrey, with Penrhyd clinging to its back and, after a startled moment, with Aurelius and Thomas in pursuit. But Thomas, mounted on the slower jennet, soon fell behind, and Aurelius was left to follow the chase by himself.

They were well out of sight of the others, around a spur of the hill and behind a great blackthorn hedge, when he caught up with her. Dismounting, he lifted her down from the palfrey, which was quietly nibbling the turf. He found her pale and composed, but trembling a little despite herself; he felt profoundly moved by it. "I would not have had this happen for the world," he said.

"It was not your fault," she replied; "it was my cousin, with his wretched slingshot."

She paused for a moment, and gave a toss to her head. "And that Thomas of Glen Daur," she said, "for encouraging him."

"Is he your young cousin's squire," asked Aurelius, "and expected to look after him?"

Penrhyd colored slightly. "He is supposed to look after me," she explained. "But so far he has not done so."

"Ah," said Aurelius in a kindly tone: "perhaps you need an older man."

He wanted to take her in his arms, but hesitated. He was fifty-one years old, and a Roman gentleman; he could not risk his dignity. His wife . . . Dame Margit . . . a guest in his house . . . Suppose she were to scream?

She had no intention of screaming. If he had put his arms around her, she would have thought it no more than kind. It did not occur to her that he could have any wish except to comfort her, and perhaps take her up on his own horse, the way her father used to do. "I have an angel," she said, "who, of course, is very much older. But he was sent to the servants' quarters."

"Ah yes," said Aurelius negligently. "That one. As I remember, he was colored like a Carthaginian."

Seeing that she had, apparently, little knowledge of history, he explained: "Carthage: a city in Africa. Destroyed by Scipio. '*Carthago delenda est.*' Long ago, I'm afraid."

"I saw him first in a dream," said Penrhyd. "Only I don't think he was so black."

"We all have our dreams," said Aurelius, moving a little closer.

"I suppose we had better go back," said Penrhyd. "Or they'll wonder where we are."

Aurelius sighed. His last thoughts were of Penrhyd's eyes, gray as rain, and her skin, white as milk. A short Saxon arrow took him between the shoulder blades, and he pitched forward on his face, just as Godwin and Thomas came pounding up the hill.

They heard Penrhyd scream once, and were in time to see her snatched from the ground by a mounted, horn-helmeted figure, tossed like a grain sack over his saddle bow, and borne away at a gallop across the field and into the woods.

"The Saxons!" cried Godwin, and wrenching his pony's head around, fled for his life down the hill to the villa, while Thomas, without thinking, flung his jennet after the raider, whipping the little donkey as far as the wood's edge. There he stopped, staring with slack jaw at the dark line of trees, while the hot rage cooled and gave way to despair. He would have thrown himself against the whole Saxon host if he could, but there was no host. There was no sound in the forest. Penrhyd was gone.

He sat listening, all his senses alert, his fingers clenching the hilt of his dagger. And little by little, in the silence, he began to feel afraid. What was he doing there, all alone on the bare hillside, with his little knife? What if the Saxons came out of the woods at him, with their ox-hide shields and their terrible throwing axes? The very lack of sound frightened him; panic rose in his throat. If they found him, he was a dead man, and Penrhyd no better for it. . . .

Fearfully, looking back over his shoulder, he made his way down the hill again to where Aurelius lay, and lifting him onto the little jennet, set out for the villa. "I must tell them," he thought. "How can I tell them?"

The Saxon who had killed Aurelius and stolen

Penrhyd had been alone. Or else he had been one of a small band of raiders; the same ones perhaps who had burned the old woman's farm. The villa's servants would be a match for them, if properly warned and prepared; Godwin would already have warned them, they only needed organizing. Did they have any stomach for fighting? Perhaps they would run away instead; perhaps they were already packing up their miserable belongings. . . .

But Penrhyd! And what of himself?—of that Thomas of Glen Daur who should have guarded her, with his life if necessary? "Sir," he had told old Anglas, "they need someone to guard them in the forest."

"You, plucker of roses?"

He wept. *"A knife is very handy for peeling turnips."*

He was not yet a man; he could not fill a man's place in the world, he could not hold what was his.

It had never been his, and it never would be. She had been right to treat him with contempt. Why hadn't he pushed on into the forest after her, at any cost? Better to be lying dead among the fallen leaves, with a Saxon arrow in his heart. . . .

Better? His throat was dry, and he felt like gagging.

"*When I saw you,*" she had said, "*you were quite quaking with fright!*"

Too late; it was too late. "Yes," he said, stumbling on down the hill, the tears running down his cheeks; "yes, I was."

CHAPTER 10

Nicias, the Greek clerk, hurrying from the villa, found Odo still in conversation with Azael, who was striving to convince him that his labors in the vineyard had not been in vain. "God gives to each," he was saying, "according to his need; and takes from each according to his ability."

"The Saxons are upon us," said the Greek, "and my Lord Aurelius is dead." So saying, he remained staring at Azael with an expression of fright.

Odo at once started up in consternation, wringing his hands. "God help us," he cried; "what has happened?" To which Nicias replied that Godwin had returned to the villa in a state of extreme perturbation, that the Lady Penrhyd had been abducted, and that Thomas the squire had disappeared. "To arms!" cried Odo. "All is lost!" And turning bitterly to Azael, he inquired:

"What kind of a guardian angel are you?"

"What difference does that make now?" demanded Nicias impatiently. "The fat is in the fire. The question is: what to do? I am inclined to let Reason be our guide, and to trust to Providence. That would be the advice of Epictetus, the great philosopher."

"It would not be the way of Paul," said Odo warmly. And he quoted from the great apostle: "'Watch ye, stand fast in the faith; quit you like men, be strong.'" And he added for Azael's benefit: "'Know ye not that we shall judge angels?'"

Azael replied that the important thing was to remain calm, and to be practical. "Let us first organize things here in the villa," he said, "after which we can see about rescuing the young lady from her ravishers."

At these words Odo turned pale, and regarded Azael with an expression of horror. "Is she to be ravished," he demanded in shocked tones, "while we sit here and do nothing?"

Azael made a helpless gesture. "I have no power to prevent it," he said. "Angels, when they take mortal form, must accept its limitations, lest they be tempted by pity or some other emotion, such as indignation, to alter the course of history."

However, he agreed, to lead them to Penrhyd's rescue, and seeing Thomas entering the yard with the jennet, on which was draped the body of Aurelius, he exclaimed:

"Let us find out what we can from this young man."

When Thomas, with many sighs and tears had told his story, Azael went to take leave of Lady Julia and Dame Margit, both of whom were pale but composed.

"It is unlikely that there will be a further attack in the immediate future," he told them, "but I have sent a message to Father Bedwyr at the Priory, telling him to see to his defenses, and asking that he send a few stout Brethren with pikes to assist in yours. I shall take with me only Thomas, and Nicias the Greek, for with a larger force we should lose the advantage of surprise."

"I shall go along with you," said Dame Margit with determination, "for I cannot think of a time in a girl's life when she would be more in need of female companionship."

Godwin also refused to stay behind. "I like riding in the forest," he said, "and hunting for enemies. When I find them, I kill them with my slingshot."

"You did little enough with your slingshot when they took your cousin," said Dame Margit indignantly.

"Well, that was different," said Godwin; "they were too far away."

"I fear that I, too, must accompany you," said the Abbot, "in order to be with my pupils, and to continue to perform my duties as a teacher. Though I admit, the spirit trembles at the prospect, and grows faint."

" 'We are troubled on every side,' " Azael declared, " 'yet not distressed; we are perplexed, but not in despair.' "

"Ah yes," said Odo more happily, recognizing the quotation: "Paul to the Corinthians."

They left the Lady Julia dry-eyed before her husband's bier. She held Aurelius's dagger in her hand, but she did not intend to use it except in extreme circumstances. "I am afraid to die," she admitted: "I am not at all like my ancestors who preferred death to dishonor, and as a result became rulers of the world."

"To take one's own life is a great sin," said Odo.

"Nonsense," said Nicias; "is it not considered a virtue to slay one's enemy?"

"It is indeed," said Odo cordially.

"Well, then," said Nicias, "is not man his own worst enemy?"

Divided in its philosophy, but united in a common resolve, the little band, led by Azael, went forth mounted with the best the villa had to offer. Azael rode a great black stallion which, standing at stud, had never been ridden before; unused to the bridle, and unfriendly to man, the savage animal knelt quietly before the angel, and waited for him to settle himself comfortably on his back. Thomas was given Aurelius's big bay, while Godwin, wearing a Roman helmet that came down over his ears, rode his own pony. Odo, mounted like Nicias on one of the villa's work horses, carried a miter borrowed from Bedwyr at the Priory; while Nicias, having possessed himself of a good-sized kitchen knife, confessed that it was mostly for use in sharpening his quill, which he had brought, along with a roll of parchment and an inkhorn, in case anything needed to be set down. "Thus," he declared, "Xenophon set out with Cyrus the Younger, and contributed a classic to literature."

Dame Margit sat her jennet as before. She had packed those simples, herbs, creams, pomades, brushes, paints, warm underthings, and a cake of soap, such as would be, she said, "most comforting to a young woman who had just suffered an experience."

As before, she had also packed the lunch, and the provisions for the campaign. This time, in addition to the plain Celtic fare of cheese, honey, coarse-ground bread, and a cold joint, she had added from the villa's storeroom some pasties, a jar of marrons, a pot of pâté and another of truffles, and a flagon of Falernian.

Arrived at the edge of the woods, they were uncertain in what direction to proceed, until a peewit flew down from its perch in a branch overhead, and lighting on Azael's wrist, pointed its beak in the direction of Thane. Taking this as a sign, Azael led the way into the forest and back along the same path by which they had come.

They had not gone very far when Nicias, aware of Dame Margit's provision for their comfort, suggested stopping for an early luncheon, a suggestion with which everyone agreed except Thomas, who was all for pressing on with all possible speed. "Even now," he exclaimed, "she may be lying lifeless upon the ground, or struggling in the arms of her captors."

"In either case," said Nicias, "we are already too late, and can do no more than extract vengeance, which we would be better able to do if fortified by a little of the pâté of the Franks, with which the pantry at the villa was well stocked."

"I too," said Odo, "would do better for a taste of the Falernian wine."

Azael, appealed to by Thomas, was also of the opinion that nothing was to be gained by hurrying. "All things are in God's hands," he said, "and He will deliver the sorrowful and the oppressed in His own time, as He did the Hebrews."

"Where are the Hebrews now?" asked Nicias.

"They are scattered all over the earth," said Azael.

"Then deliver me," said Nicias, "from a like deliverance!"

"I cannot see to get the food to my mouth," said Godwin, "because of my helmet."

"Then take it off," said Dame Margit, "and eat."

"Take it off?" cried Godwin indignantly. "What if we were to be attacked? I have to be ready for anything."

"Then I shall have to feed you," said his nurse.

"I should like a pasty," said Godwin, "some cheese, a beaker of cow's milk, and a marron."

While Godwin was being fed, Nicias set himself to discuss philosophy with Azael. "You say that you are an angel," he remarked. "Tell me, then: what do you do?"

"I do God's errands on earth," replied Azael.

"The gods also have messengers," declared Nicias, "in whom they confide."

"I am not in God's confidence," said Azael stiffly; "I merely do what I am told."

"And who, then, guards the world?" asked Nicias.

"The Archangels," said Azael.

"They do not do a very good job of it," said Nicias.

"What I desire," he continued, "is the simple and transquil enjoyment of life. There is an inner world, and an outer world; from either can come delight. But I hold that it can also come from both together, in saying which I believe that I go further than the philosopher Marcus Aurelius."

"And are you so proud of that?" asked Azael.

"Of course," replied Nicias simply; "although I do not expect it to make me famous. I have only a small talent, which age with its fading powers has reduced still further. However, for a philosopher to be the first to express a profound thought, however trifling, is a reason for pride of some kind."

"Do you not know," said Azael, "that in the end the last shall be first, and the meek shall inherit the earth?"

Nicias made a gesture of distaste. "Such a thought offends me," he said, "as it must any seeker after perfection. What a broth of mediocrity! Fortunately I shall not be alive to see it. A man should have the right to aspire, and not be obliged to diminish himself. For man is unique, and beautiful, and beloved of the gods; in his pain and grief, and among the disasters of history, he still preserves within himself the seeds of happiness, and of love."

"Love," said Odo, breaking into the conversation, "does not emanate from man, but from God. Is that not so, Azael?"

The angel hesitated a moment before replying. "I do not know very much about love," he said at last, "for it is a term which in the old days was not much used in heaven."

CHAPTER 11

Slung across the Saxon's saddle bow, Penrhyd
was carried off into the forest. Except for that one
scream, she was too frightened to make a sound,
for she expected the most terrible things to happen to her without having any idea what they
might be. She thought that she would certainly
be killed, but death was something she couldn't
picture for herself; what she feared was all that
would surely lead up to it, pain like the time she

had fallen and skinned her knee, or perhaps worse,
perhaps even much worse, worse than anything
she could imagine. And there was the immediate
terror of not being able to breathe, with her nose
pressed against the horse's rough, shaggy flank,
and the way she was lying with her head hanging
down on one side and her legs on the other. To be
so helpless . . . not to be a person any more, not
to be a young lady, but a thing, a rag flung across
a horse's back. . . . To be so humiliated. . . .

A picture flashed through her mind, of how she
had once stepped on a spider, and how the little
insect's legs had curled and twisted in a panic,
not knowing what had happened to it, or why, or
what to do, or how to escape, or whom to cry to.
She understood that panic now. Even with an
Abbot, a guardian angel, even with a mother in
Ireland, a girl could be reaped, and the world
come to an end, and all Britain go down into
darkness—and no one to cry to.

Where was Azael? And Thomas . . . Ah,
Thomas! He had failed her again. But this time
there was no nosegay waiting for her; this time
there was nothing waiting—or worse than noth-

ing. She would never see Thomas again, nor he her; it was over, it was all finished, everything was over.

The man above her was singing, a wild, strange song, and with a sound of sadness in it. It made her want to cry; she felt suddenly a great pity for herself, and for Thomas of Glen Daur; she saw him in her mind's eye, calling her name through the lonely silence of the world, and she longed to comfort him. "Dear Thomas," she murmured, "dear heart, do not weep," . . . and wept, for herself and for the world, her nose buried in the horse's hair. For some reason it seemed to do her good, and her mind drifted off into emptiness. She thought that she slept a little.

She came back to life again, aware of other men and horses around her, of rough, guttural voices speaking a language she did not understand. They seemed merry. . . . She could smell the strong meadow smell of the horse under her, and the sour smell of the man above, an odor compounded of rank fur, fermented honey, tanned hides, and unwashed flesh. There was also,

strangely enough, a smell of cow's horns, and sea-
weed.

Then there was no sound but the trampling of
hooves, the creak of leather, the swish of branches,
and an occasional shout from one of the raiders,
which was answered by her captor.

She moved uncomfortably, kicking feebly with
her feet, and he lifted her by the hair and set her
upright on the horse in front of him. She looked
at him through tears of pain and outrage; and
thought that she must have seen him before in a
bad dream. He wore a leather shirt and the great
horned helmet of the Saxon host; his eyes were
like moonstones, his hair the color of bleached
flax. His teeth were blackened, and some missing;
and his breath smelled of boiled eels.

If it was her first look at him, it was also his
first real look at her; and to her astonishment, his
face fell, and he said something to his companions
which caused them to shout with laughter. Penrhyd turned rigid, and drew in her breath; what
were they laughing at? Was it at her? A terrible
feeling of humiliation made her shake as though

with ague; and in a sudden access of rage and despair, she turned on the grinning Saxon and beat at him with her fists. "Let me go!" she cried. "Let me go! You horrible, horrible . . ."

He gawked at her for a moment, and then brought his hand in a great backhanded swing across her face. It knocked her dizzy; she toppled, clutched at nothing, and fell with a strangled gasp onto the ground beneath the horse's hooves.

He reined in, then, and sat looking down at her. He saw a scrawny girl with mousy hair and closed eyes, and a red weal across her cheek; and he wondered why he had bothered carrying her off at all. She was obviously good for nothing, neither for work in the yard, nor for pleasure in bed. She was of no use to a man, and so of no value to anybody.

Lazily, almost indifferently, he raised his seaxe, the sharp, curved throwing axe of the war host; it would split her cleanly between the breasts, but he would have to dismount to pick it up again. It was scarcely worth the trouble.

His companions had gone on ahead. Alone for a moment, he stared down at her and she stared back, her gray eyes wide and bright with defiance. As he hesitated, a peewit flew suddenly past his head, and without thinking, as though he were brushing away a wasp, he swung his axe at the bird, cutting it in half. The sudden gesture caused his horse to bound forward, leaving the girl on the ground behind him, and he ripped out an oath. "Thunderweather!" he grunted. "Woden curse it!" But she was out of range, and all at once he no longer cared. "Let it be," he thought. "Food for the wolves."

He was aware of the forest's silence all around him, a silence like a sound withheld. A forest was a fearsome place for a man alone; there were more than wolves there. "By Freya," he muttered, "I am far from home."

And setting heels to his horse, he followed his companions, halooing to them as he went.

Penrhyd lay still for a long time, letting the fright drain out of her body, leaving it cold and limp; waiting for the too rapid beating of her heart to slow, waiting to get her breath again. After a while she got wearily and shakily to her feet, and gathered up the two bloody bits of the peewit; she felt vaguely that she ought to be grateful to the little bird, and should bury it, but before she had taken more than a step, she was sick, and vomited, and was left retching and gasping and racked by dry sobs.

There was no way to stop them; her mind was a blank. When they let up at last, she rose from her knees, and looked about her. "I must get back to the villa," she thought drearily. "They'll be wondering where I am."

She started walking, stumbling over roots, catching her tunic and her unbound hair in the bushes. She was no longer on the path, she couldn't find it anywhere. Where the villa was, in what direction, she didn't know.

She walked for a long time, resting now and then on a bed of moss or against the trunk of a tree. She found water in a spring among some ferns, and used it to bathe the bruise on her cheek. As the day drew to a close and the light in the forest dimmed, she began to think of the dangers of the dark, of wolves and bears, gryfons, basilisks, and manticores. "I must find a tree," she thought, "and climb into a branch, to save my life."

She found an old oak, not knowing that it was sacred to the Druids, and scrambling up into it, settled herself in the crotch of a large limb. For a while she watched the forest shadows, her heart beating at every sound; but she saw nothing, and presently, as night set in, she lay back against the rough bark of the tree and closed her eyes. She was too tired to think about herself any more; and after saying her prayers, drifted off to sleep. Her last thoughts were of her mother, and Ireland across the sea, where the sun went down, all in the green of evening and the rose of dusk. Sleeping, she wept.

In the dark hours of the night a great white owl swooped silently down and landed in the tree beside her. Its weight, which depressed the branch, did not waken her. It held a rabbit in its beak, which it ate; then sliding quietly along the branch toward the sleeping girl, it leaned its soft wing against her face.

At daybreak the great bird flew away, leaving

Penrhyd dreaming; in her dream she was at Nairn again, her own home, and her father was coming to take her for a ride on his horse. But when he appeared, he had Thomas's face, and an arrow through his breast.

She woke in the gray dawn, with an owl's feather in her hair, to find a little bowl on the branch beside her, fashioned from a leaf, and filled with cool water, and on another leaf a handful of blackberries. Surprised, but convinced that she was in God's hands, she gave thanks, and climbing down from her perch, proceeded on her way through the forest. She failed to see on the ground beneath the tree in which she had spent the night, the footprints of a ferocious manticore. She thought that her friends must be near, and that she would soon find them.

She was mistaken. Coming out of the woods at midday, she found herself upon a bare, wind-swept moor, with the cloud-scattered sky above her and wave after wave of rolling forest fading off into the blue distance. Where the moor rose to its highest point stood a circle of twelve great stones, keeping watch over the countryside like huge sentinels, gray, silent, and old as time. And within the circle, on a round stone inscribed with the ancient sign of the sun, sat an old woman, dressed in ragged green. Her long, gray hair, topped by a chaplet of moon daisies, hung straggling down her back, and she carried a basket of woven rushes and a gilded sickle. "Well," she said: "these are strange times, when children walk alone in the forest!"

And peering at Penrhyd nearsightedly, she inquired:

"What brings you here, child?"

Penrhyd bobbed her a curtsy. "I am lost," she said. "I was taken by Saxons, and am seeking my friends, the Abbot of Swynneddfod and Azael, my guardian angel."

The old woman gave a sniff, and wiped her nose with her sleeve. "An Abbot and an angel," she said bitterly. "You are one of those called Christians, and you have no business here at all. I should not have spoken to you, except for the white owl's feather in your hair."

"I have no idea how it got there," said Penrhyd apologetically. "And I am only trying to find my way to Malmesbury Priory."

The old woman waved her sickle menacingly in the air. "I have no knowledge of Priories," she said. And gazing sternly at the girl, she added:

"You do not know who I am?"

"No," said Penrhyd, "though I take you to be a noble lady."

"I am the Druidess of the Corn God," said the old woman, and gave her a proud look.

Penrhyd drew back in alarm, for she had heard the women of her mother's house speak in hushed tones of the Corn God, who, next to Lud himself, was the most fearful of all the Ancient Ones. "I am glad to see that you have heard of me," said the Druidess, noting her sudden recoil, "but there is no reason to be frightened. I am not here in my official capacity. As a matter of fact, I was simply sitting down and taking a little rest from my work."

And she held up the basket, which was half full of mistletoe. "The old legs are not what they used to be," she said.

"When I was a child," said Penrhyd, taking heart, "and before I was brought to Holy Writ, I was told that to see the Corn God was to die."

The priestess waved her sickle again, in a friendlier manner. "Not at this time of year," she said; and she added thoughtfully:

"Are you afraid of death?"

"Yes," said Penrhyd simply. "Since yesterday."

The Druidess sighed deeply. "You should not be afraid," she said. "From death comes life. That is one of the mysteries."

"Our Lord died," said Penrhyd, "that we might live."

"Every god must die," said the old woman, "and be born again; why else do you think we light the fires at Beltane? Your lord is no different from anybody else."

"Odo would tell you differently," thought Penrhyd, but she did not say so. She had no desire to enter into a discussion for which she was ill-prepared. "If you cannot tell me where to find Malmesbury," she said, her voice beginning to tremble a little, "at least tell me where I can find shelter and a crust of bread, for I am lost and weary and very hungry." And with that, she burst into tears.

The old priestess hesitated, frowned, clucked,

and bit her lip. "Ah, well," she said at last regret-
fully, "one cannot always choose the things that
happen to one." And in a brisker tone, she declared: "You can come with me if you like. I
have only a small bothy, but I dare say I can
find a corner for you to lie down in."

As she led the way across the moor, her ragged
green gown trailing on the ground and catching
in the furze and the brambles, she remarked:
"You were right in thinking that I am of noble
birth, for my grandfather was Arch Druid of all
Britain, on the maternal side. But between Patrick
in Ireland and Merdin being locked up in a tree
by the witch Nimue, and what with first the
Romans and then the Saxons knocking over our
holy places, we of the Old People have fallen on
hard times."

She stopped in front of a low mud hut, roofed
with turf and rounded like a barrow. "No doubt
you're used to better," she said, "but you're welcome, for what it is." And stepping across the
threshold, she held back the heavy hide which
served as a curtain at the door. "What is your

name, child?" she asked. "Or should I call you
Owl Feather?"

"I was Penrhyd of Nairn," said the girl, "and
then of Thane, but it is all gone up in flames, and
I am on my way to Malmesbury or to Ireland,
where my grandmother was married to a King."

"Penrhyd," mused the priestess: "a good Celtic
name. And the grandmother married across the
sea. Well, come in, child, come in."

And patting Penrhyd on the shoulder, she ushered her into a small, round room lighted only by
its smoke hole in the roof. Fat lamps hung from
the rough beams, as well as strings of onions,
peppers, and bags of dried herbs, and a great copper cauldron hung suspended over the fire in
which some of last night's coals were still glowing red among the ashes. A spinning wheel stood
in the middle of the room beside the hearth,
where it could catch the light of the smoke hole;
and in the shadows to the rear, Penrhyd saw an
iron-bound chest overflowing with silks and linens
in scarlet and gold, bracelets of bronze, necklaces
and earrings of copper, and colored shells. On the

hearthstone itself lay a sharp bronze knife, two bowls, and the severed head and entrails of a mouse, in which the priestess had been studying the day's auguries.

There was some yellow broom and sweet fern spread out against the wall, and she told Penrhyd that this was where she might sleep. "But first," she said, "let me get you something to eat."

With her eyes on the dead mouse, Penrhyd shook her head. "Oh no," she said; "really not. I'm not at all . . . madam . . . lady . . ."

"Nonsense," said the Druidess, giving her a hearty clap between the shoulder blades. "A nice bowl of broth, and a bite of cheese—

"And you may call me by my name," she said, "which is Granni."

CHAPTER 12

The peewit did not return to Azael, and the little
band of rescuers, without guidance, and taking
the wrong turn in the forest, were soon far from
both Penrhyd asleep in her tree and Malmesbury,
where the serfs and villeins stood to arms during
the night awaiting an attack which never came.
When darkness made further progress impossible,
Azael called a halt, ordered Nicias to light a fire,
and set Thomas to act as sentry a little beyond

the circumference of the firelight. "Report to me," he told him, "if you hear anything suspicious."

"I am already half asleep," said Thomas, "being worn out with the events of the day. Would it not be better if you kept watch yourself?"

"I shall visit you from time to time," said Azael, "like Gideon at the Well of Harod. Try to stay awake." To which Nicias added: "Alexander the Great, who also slept badly, did not post himself as sentry, but remained in his tent surrounded by his loves, both men and women." At this Dame Margit blushed, but it was hidden from the others by the darkness.

"I wonder at you," she said, casting an anxious glance in Godwin's direction, "talking like that in front of the child."

"I thought we were an army," said Nicias, "not a *schola puerorum.*"

Toward midnight Thomas fell asleep, as expected, and a small green snake, attracted by the warmth of his body, crept into his lap, where it curled itself up in comfort. Each time that Azael came by on his rounds of inspection, the tiny creature hid its head in the folds of Thomas's tunic, while faint, far-off memories of Divine Wrath echoed like thunder in the dim cell chambers of its brain. In the early dawn, the little serpent went off to find its own meal of bugs and other small creatures, and Thomas awoke in time for breakfast, refreshed and eager for the expedition to be on its way.

All that day they traveled through the forest in the general direction of Thane, where they thought the Saxon host to be encamped; and at nightfall found themselves once more at the old woman's burned-out farmstead on the nearer side of the great moor. Seeing again the little wooden doll which Penrhyd had held in her arms, Dame Margit burst into tears, and even Azael was moved to murmur something about a happier occasion.

"And yet," said Nicias, "all things are relative, both to one another and to the whole; and what at one moment may seem to us the height of suffering, or even boredom, often appears later to have been the best of times, comparatively speaking."

"That is true," said Odo, "for I have sometimes thought that to have been present at the Crucifixion must surely be the greatest happiness that one could wish for in the world, yet had I been there at the time I am not sure that I would have enjoyed it."

"So you're back again," said the old woman; "what did you bring for lunch?"

Dame Margit unpacked the provisions, and they shared pâté de foie gras, gherkins, marrons, a cold galantine of beef, slices of tongue, and a stuffed capon with their hostess, whose contribution to the feast was a jar of water from the well, for which she charged Odo five denarii. "One cannot give things away for nothing," she said; "not these days."

"God gives His grace to all," said Odo, "at all times, and for nothing." The old woman gazed around her at her burned and shattered home. "Not to me, He didn't," she said, reaching for the pickles.

However, she did tell them that the Fair, which had been at Llangford, and had left that place to escape the oncoming Saxons, was now encamped in the Great Meadow on the far side of the moor, which they remembered for having crossed it on their way to Malmesbury. "Then we shall be on our way," said Azael, "for we may find news of our friend among the soothsayers and magicians of the carnival."

"I cannot imagine," said Nicias, "why you, who claim to be in the employ of a god, should wish to consult a soothsayer."

"Saul consulted the witches of Endor," said Azael. "And it is generally true that in matters of this sort it is wise to seek all the help one can get."

"The ancient Greeks," said Nicias, "addressed their inquiries to the oracle of Apollo, at Delphi."

"I flew over it," said Azael, "and below the temple there was only an empty hole in some rocks, from which issued an odorous vapor."

"And what," asked Nicias impudently, "was in the Ark at Jerusalem?"

"It wasn't gas, at any rate," said Azael.

They found the Fair, as the old woman had told them, in the Great Meadow on the far side of the moor. The animal cages with their solid wheels were lined up at one end of the Midway, the booths of the hucksters and magicians in between, while tests of skill and games of chance

were held at the other end, which boasted a catapult and a pavilion where, under bright colored
flags and pennants, such delicacies as pigs' knuck-
les, boiled cabbage, metheglin, heather beer, herring, and wine from Gaul could be purchased for
a few denarii or a Saxon skeatta.

As the companions drew near, they were surprised to see that they were not the only visitors
to the Fair, for already a number of persons, both
male and female, had gathered to gape and gawk
at the animals, to buy a fairing, or to drink a
beaker of heather beer. "Where do you think they
come from?" said Odo in wonderment. "For there
is not a town or hamlet to my knowledge within a
day's journey, in any direction."

"Wherever there is a carnival," said Nicias
wisely, "there are people attracted to it like in-
sects, of which it was said that the male lunar
moth will fly as far as twenty leagues to find its
mate, attracted by the odor."

"Yes indeed," said Odo, sniffing the aroma of
boiled cabbage in the air, "it is indescribable."

However, no one at the Fair had seen the Saxons, or heard their hunting horns, and it was

thought that they might have avoided Thane altogether, and headed south to join a larger raiding party which was known to be working in the
vicinity of Dartmoor. "For had they been return-
ing to Thane," said the head animal keeper, an
African of the Baluba tribe, "we must have passed
them as we came up from Llangford, and have
been aware of it by the trumpeting of the elephant."

"Is that what it is?" asked Thomas, examining
the huge beast with admiration; "I thought it was
a wyvern."

"The wyvern," said the keeper, "is over there;
as you can see, it is half bird and half beast, it has
a long neck and horned claws, runs at an exces-
sive speed, and upon being alarmed hides its
head in the sand."

"No doubt in that position it prays," said Odo;
"an edifying manifestation of faith."

Godwin, meanwhile, had discovered what he
took to be the unicorn, a huge black animal with
a leathery hide and a single great horn sticking
up from its nose. "I am glad I am not a maiden,"
Godwin thought, "having to take that in my lap":

and drawing his slingshot, let fly at the beast's ribs. The shot had no effect; it was doubtful that the unicorn even felt it. "I shall do better against gryfons," thought Godwin.

And going off in search of Dame Margit, whom he found in front of a booth devoted to colored ribbons and necklaces of shell and amber, he remarked: "I'm hungry."

"Not now," said Dame Margit, holding a square of color against her hair to study the effect; "you just had your lunch."

"That old woman ate most of it," said Godwin morosely.

"So she did," said Dame Margit, "and you'd ought to be ashamed of yourself, for a more uncharitable and un-Christian remark I cannot imagine."

"Can I have a pig's knuckle?" asked Godwin.

"No," she said.

The head keeper approached Azael, followed at a decent interval by his three helpers, their black skins glistening in the sunlight.

"Tell me, brother," he said in the KiBira dialect, "what are you doing here with these white folk? And were are you from?"

Although Azael did not speak any African language except the Ethiopian, he understood the keeper's question, and replied in Latin: "I am from heaven, and I am here on my Father's business."

"From which part of heaven are you?" asked the keeper: "The Congo? Or the Sudan? Or is your father a great chief among the Masai?"

"I am an angel," said Azael simply.

The head keeper drew back in alarm. "A black angel?" he exclaimed in disbelief; "you know there never was a black angel. Black angels are white."

And turning to his helpers, he declared: "This man is a ju-ju."

At once they uttered a wail and hurried off, their heads hidden in their arms. "Why do you come here?" demanded the head keeper, backing away; "did I ever harm your ancestors?"

Azael sighed deeply. "You have no cause to fear me," he said; "rather, you should rejoice that God saw fit to make me black, like yourself. Are you, a keeper of elephants, not the equal of those around you?"

The Baluba shook his head gloomily. "In my own country," he said, "I was a warrior; I slew many men, cut off their heads, and ate their brains, hearts, and testicles. That is the manly thing to do. Here I shovel elephant dung, which would be all right if I were a Pygmy, but I am not a Pygmy."

"It is written," said Azael, "that the meek shall inherit the earth."

"All the meek will inherit," said the Bantu, "is elephant dung."

And as Azael turned sadly away, he added angrily:

"Who wants to be equal? The Ashanti? The Watusi? To be equal is something for termites. Where I come from, the onliest thing everybody wants to be is superior!"

CHAPTER 13

In Cador's high-timbered hall at Isca, the Prince of Cornwall sat at meat surrounded by his hearth companions and warriors, his harpers, and his dogs. Now that the Romans were gone, and Roman ways no longer in fashion, many of the Cymric nobles had returned to the old ways, and wore their hair and beards long; and women were not seen at formal banquets any more, except to pass the meats and keep the horn cups filled. Cador himself wore the circlet of Irish gold in his hair that tokened a Prince of the Cymri, as well as the gold armband above the elbow, and the great brooch of amethyst set in silver, which served to pin his tartan cloak at the shoulder.

In the smoky, high-ceilinged hall with its painted walls lit by candles and warmed by the blazing hearth fire, Cador addressed his guests, the Abbot of Swynneddfod, Nicias the philosopher, and Thomas of Glen Daur. Azael was also present, seated well below the salt, among the harpers and soothsayers, potters, bead-makers, and beer-brewers; but Dame Margit and Godwin had been sent to the ladies' quarters, to Godwin's embarrassment.

As the Prince spoke, sparrows flew about among the smoke-stained roofbeams, and boar hounds snapped at one another among the rushes beneath the table. "There are no Saxons hereabouts," said Cador; "they know better than to show themselves at Isca, for the Celts have always been invincible at war."

"We were not invincible at Salisbury Plain," said Odo in a low voice to Nicias.

"No," said Nicias, "nor at the fall of Caractcus."

"Ah well," said Odo, "I suppose one must keep one's spirits up."

"It is unusual," said Cador, "to have the company of an Abbot and a philosopher at our table, both at the same time; and I look forward to the good conversation which we will enjoy. For I must tell you that I am also something of a Christian, and a philosopher, although I must admit I am not yet altogether comfortable in my Christianity, it being so new in the world."

And addressing Odo, he inquired:

"How old is Our Lord, Jesus Christ?"

"Five hundred and seventy-five years," replied Odo, "more or less, depending on the exact date of Our Lord's birth, which is, unfortunately, unknown. However, it is believed that He was thirty-three years of age when He ascended to heaven."

"Well, there you are," said Cador uncomfortably: "Lud is at least a thousand years older."

He sighed, and stroked his long, fox-colored beard. "Just the same," he admitted, "I consider God the Father, the Son, and all the Saints a more impressive array than our own Tyr, Lud, and

Ruanh of the Long Hair. I am particularly fond of the angels, who, I am told, sweep through the skies with bright wings and flaming swords."

"You have such an angel at your table," said Odo boldly. "He is seated below the salt."

Cador stared at Azael in surprise. "Do you mean that one?" he asked, pointing. "But he is black! And neither winged nor shining."

"Nevertheless," said Odo, "he is a veritable angel, such as will accompany your soul to heaven."

The Prince's face fell. "I am not sure that I should be happy in heaven, under those circumstances," he said doubtfully. "I would prefer, rather, the Elysian Fields, where, to be sure, I should find myself among foreigners, but of a complexion not unlike my own; or better yet, the Blessed Isles of our Celtic heroes, with Niamh of the White Hands to minister to my comfort."

Raising his ribbed gold cup to his mouth, he took a long swallow of honey beer, while his followers lifted their drinking horns and did the same. At once the oldest harper struck up a song in praise of Innogen, the daughter of Cunobelin, whose chastity had survived countless perils and the advances of a Frenchman.

When the song was ended, Cador set down his cup and wiped the foam from his beard with the back of his hand. Peering again at Azael at the end of the table, he set his face in a frown. "Sir Abbot," he said, "see to it that when my time comes, I am accompanied to heaven by a proper angel, having his wings, and wearing the gold circlet of a Celtic Prince, which you call a halo, on his head."

"Have no fear," said Azael quietly; "you will be properly attended to."

"How would you choose to die, philosopher," asked Cador, turning to Nicias, "since, unlike myself, you are not likely to die in battle."

"Why," said Nicias modestly, "I should like to die gracefully, without pain or fear. But since I have, after all, no choice of death, but must take what comes, I prefer to think rather of how I would like to live, conformably with nature, virtuous and free of passion, in the simple and tranquil enjoyment of life."

"That is a good way to live, certainly," agreed Cador, "but where are we to find virtue today? What man can boast of the devotion of a wife like Innogen, who loved her husband even in misfortune?"

"It is true," thought Thomas disconsolately, "women have no sympathy for a man who has fallen into the water." And from his undistinguished place at the table, he leaned forward and exclaimed:

"Arthur will rise again!"

At once a hush fell on the hall, as everyone turned to look at him, while a subdued stir ran around the table. "Why do you say that, young man?" asked Cador, frowning. But Thomas was suddenly silent, tongue-tied and embarrassed. Why had he said it, indeed? He did not know. Perhaps because of the pain at seeing a childhood hero die.

It was Nicias, the philosopher, who answered for him. As much at home, because of his philosophy, in a palace as in a hovel, he expounded his ideas with quiet dignity. "All heroes rise again," he said, "though not necessarily in the flesh; but whether for a long time, or for only a short time, history alone decides. Our only means of judging greatness is whether it survives. Immortality on earth—for I am not speaking of the hereafter, whether it be spent in heaven or in the Elysian Fields—is to be found only in men's memories and regard. When a man dies, he is first mourned, and then forgotten in favor of men still living; yet after a while his name and nature and his deeds begin to stir awake in men's minds, and so he may be born again for a second time, less in the flesh, but greater in reverence and love. How long this resurrected existence endures, determines his greatness: thus we count as truly great Aristotle and Epictetus, but who remembers Phidias and Aristophanes? And whereas Julius Caesar and Alexander of Macedon are renowned for their exploits, and have statues of themselves in public places, and Hadrian is remembered for his wall, who today salutes the ghosts of Ovid, Virgil, or Horace?" "Perhaps they will waken tomorrow," said the old harper timidly, "or the day after." "They will never rise again," said Nicias with finality. "We have left them behind us."

"You do not consider my ancestor Cunobelin to be immortal?" asked Cador ominously.

"Only through his daughter Innogen," replied Nicias, "and only so long as the harpers remember the tune."

Confused and unhappy, Thomas of Glen Daur barely listened to the philosopher's thoughtful and dignified exposition. The defeat of Arthur, which had upset the world, had not until then touched him very deeply, or in more than a general way; now suddenly, without knowing why, he was experiencing a feeling of intense melancholy combined with a sense of personal loss which at first he failed to understand. With Arthur gone, Britain was gone; of what use were the clans, for the most part quarreling among themselves, the chieftains plotting for power, the princes like this Cador, whose warriors, for all their long hair and fierce looks, would go down like wheat before the scythes of the war host?

All would soon be over, and Britain vanquished once again, by a darker and more barbarous foe than Rome. He saw her where she lay, prostrate beneath the Saxon heel; but her face was the face of Penrhyd. Pale, weary, and streaked with tears, it was turned up in resignation to the conqueror.

Thomas uttered a groan; and the warrior at his side, whose name was Gwyn, and whose tartan was hooked to his shoulder with a great bronze pin, gazed at him anxiously. "Are you ill, friend?" he inquired solicitously; "if so, try not to turn in my direction, for my tunic is new, and cost me two gold pieces."

"I am ill only in spirit," said Thomas, "for the maiden to whom I pledged my faith was taken from me by the Saxons, and lies, like Britain, in extremity."

"Our swords will save Britain," said Gwyn, "but I cannot promise you anything for your maiden, who will have to rely on your own sword and that of her relatives, or a large ransom, or some witchcraft or other from the Druids."

"She has no relatives," said Thomas gloomily, "beyond a mother in Ireland; and I have no sword, only a dagger for peeling turnips, with which I suppose I could kill myself."

"Do not do that," exclaimed the warrior earnestly, "for you would miss all the best things of life, the banquets, the singing, and the battles, to say nothing of Midsummer Eve with its fires and willing damsels to go with you into the bushes. And then there is always something to look forward to, like meeting your maiden again in happier circumstances."

"Ah," said Thomas, "would it were so."

"As for a sword," said Gwyn, "I have two; you can have one of them for the price of a new hat."

"Alas," groaned Thomas, "I have no money."

"A jewel, then," said Gwyn, "worth a few silver pieces?"

"I have no jewel either," said Thomas; "but I have a featherbed, or at least I know where I can lay my hands on one."

"A featherbed would be very comfortable on a long campaign," said Gwyn thoughtfully, "or for sleeping at night in winter. Very well, it is a bargain between us: a sword for a featherbed."

"I shall have to talk to Dame Margit first," said Thomas uneasily; "wait for me outside the hall."

In the women's quarters, Dame Margit and Godwin had settled down for the night. "I do not see why I cannot have an angel of my own," said Godwin, "instead of a nurse."

"Why, I am sure you might have," said Dame Margit, unfastening the pins in her hair; "and you have only to ask for her."

"Her?" exclaimed Godwin; "I had not thought to have another woman to look after me."

"What else?" asked Dame Margit sensibly. "Seeing as how your cousin drew a man, and black at that, though when it came right down to it, he was of no more use than a goose." The good woman's eyes filled with tears. "Ah dear, the poor child," she sighed, "where is she now?It is enough to make a body doubt God Himself, the saints forgive me!"

"If Odo heard you, he would be marvelously put out," said Godwin, "and I think I do not want an angel after all."

When Thomas arrived to ask Dame Margit for the featherbed, Godwin was already asleep in it, and Dame Margit at her prayers. "I wouldn't think of it," she said; "it is out of the question, and I wonder at you even suggesting it."

"It is not for me," said Thomas, "but for your charge, whose very life is at stake."

"My charge is sleeping in it," said the nurse, "as you can see, with his thumb in his mouth."

"I am not speaking of young Master Godwin," said Thomas, "but of the Lady Penrhyd." At this Dame Margit burst again into tears, and Thomas hastened to press his advantage. "Had I worn a sword that day at Malmesbury Moor," he said, "I should have rescued her or died in the attempt."

"I am sure of it," sobbed the unhappy woman. "Ah me!"

"I would even have withstood the boar," said Thomas, "had I been sword in hand."

"I do not doubt it," she said. "But the nights are cold here in Cornwall, and I would miss the warmth of it."

"They are colder in Anderida," said Thomas, "or in Tanatus, where the great burg of Hengist is said to be located, and Penrhyd without a cover for her thin frame."

At this the poor woman's tears flowed faster than ever. "It is her own featherbed," she cried, "and I have been enjoying it, while she shivers in some Saxon's wattled hut. I am ashamed to feel my own warm feet." And seizing one corner of the fatted quilt, she gave it a fierce tug. "Out, Godwin, out!" she cried. "You have lived long enough in comfort, and so have I!" So saying, she tumbled the sleeping boy out onto the ground, where he snored no less loudly than before; and lifting the featherbed in her arms, pressed it against Thomas's chest. "Take it!" she said. "And may goose feathers prevail where the wings of angels could not."

In the great hall, at the far end of the table, Azael sat with bowed head. He knew himself to be an object of pity on the part of some of the company, and of derision on the part of others; but he was used to it. It was not easy to be an angel, and to be obliged always to avoid direct action, if possible. But he was not used to being so disliked, and he felt sad because he did not know why. Was it only because he was black? But many fine and beautiful things were black: a tarn under a windy sky, a harp of polished bog oak, the gleam of obsidian . . .

"Look'ee, fellow," said the old harper, leaning

forward, "if you'm a nangel, like 'ee say, you'm magic of a sort, na? Why waste time fighting, if you'm power to split men's skulls wi' a word?"

Azael remained silent. Of what use to tell the old man that he had no such magic; that what power he had came to him by appointment only? "Oh," he thought, "if I could show myself in God's true glory; if only once I could assume my heavenly form and shelter some poor wretch beneath my wings!"

But he knew it was impossible. Without being given leave to do so, he had no right to invoke the power of heaven; without permission, he dared not involve it in events. "I was not sent here," he said, "to meddle with history."

Had he, perhaps, already meddled too much?

CHAPTER 14

Rain swept in from the gray Atlantic over the fens
and the marshes, over the dark woods and the
open moors. In Cambria the Vale of Arfon was
loud with water, mourning Arthur's passing; and
Snowden hid its face in the clouds. Piling east-
ward the cold rain fell on the blackened ruins of
Thane and Swynneddfod, on Malmesbury Priory
and Cador's host at Isca. Britain was all a mist of
water, and no one abroad; the Saxons at home

before their fires, and Penrhyd indoors in Granni's
bothy busy with household tasks.

"You could not have been brought up very
well," said Granni, "for you have no grace with a
broom at all."

"I am sorry," said Penrhyd, wiping the perspira-
tion from her forehead, "but I was brought up in
a castle, where others swept the floors and cooked
the meats."

"That is nothing to be proud of," said the Druidess; "my ancestors lived here long before there
were such things as castles, and did their own
work, including auguries, and human sacrifices to
the gods."

"Human?" asked Penrhyd in a muffled voice.

"Indeed yes," said Granni with relish; "there
has never been anything better than the roasted
heart of a child or a maiden to please Old
Lud. . . ."

Lifting Penrhyd from the floor where she had
fallen in a faint, the old priestess fanned the girl's
face and sprinkled it with water. "Now then,"
she scolded, "whatever would you want to go
and do a thing like that for?"

"I am so sorry," murmured Penrhyd feebly. "I was only dizzy for a moment."

"You're not sick or anything?" asked Granni suspiciously. "The morning sickness perhaps?"

"Whatever is that?" asked Penrhyd.

"Ah well," said the Druidess; "if you don't know . . ." She placed her wrinkled hand for a moment on the girl's abdomen. "You're not pregnant, are you?" she demanded.

Penrhyd stared at her in astonishment. "How could I be," she remarked, "seeing that I am maiden, and unmarried?"

The old priestess studied her for a while with a curious gleam in her eye. Beltane was coming. It had been a long time since a virgin had been sacrificed to Lud. . . .

On the other hand, a pretty girl could be very useful, not only around the house, but where money was to be made, as at the Fair during the Midsummer Festival. For Granni, priestess that she was, was not above doing a bit of fortune-telling; not the ordinary kind, with stones and a bowl of water, but with the old spells and incantations, the right side and the left side of a mouse's spleen or a fowl's gizzard. . . . She had often noticed the brightly dressed girls with hoops of gold or silver in their ears, outside the tents of the soothsayers and necromancers, whose talents, she assured Penrhyd, were child's play compared to her own.

"That is," she said, "if ever I were to rear back and let loose. But they do attract the men. Tell me, my dear—have you ever done one of those Carthaginian dances?"

"No, ma'am," said Penrhyd, "but I have done the fling, the reel, run-sheep-run, the quadrille, and the pavilion."

"I wonder how you would look in a colored shawl," said Granni.

"I also learned the Irish cakewalk as a child," said Penrhyd, "to please my mother."

As she stirred the ashes of the fire, her eyes grew misty. "I often wonder if I shall ever see her again," she said, and a tear fell onto the hearth.

"You miss your mother, do you not?" said Granni.

"She was kind and beautiful," said Penrhyd, "and she loved me very much."

"It's a wonder she didn't take you with her then," said Granni.

"It was thought I would be better off with my uncle Thane," said Penrhyd, "than among the rough men of Armagh."

"We Druids are very strong in Ireland," said Granni, "though I do not altogether trust the Fenian branch."

She taught Penrhyd to sweep and clean, to lay the fire and draw the water, to grind the corn, bake the bannocks, and clean out the bird cage. "A bird is a great comfort on winter nights," said Granni.

"Surely," said Penrhyd, "by winter my angel will have found me."

"I have heard of these angels," said Granni; "they are said to be creatures with wings, like the gryfon, but with human faces."

"Mine has a human face," said Penrhyd, "but it is black, and because of that he was sent to the servants' quarters, and so was not with me when Aurelius was killed and I was taken."

"Perhaps he is not an angel at all," said Granni, "but a demon. Have you thought of that?"

And she explained to Penrhyd that a sprig of mistletoe cut with a golden sickle, and the heart of a toad, with hyssop, coriander, and wild thyme brewed together, would free her from any demon in the world. "It would do no harm to try it," she said.

Going to the chest behind the hearth, she rummaged in it for her golden sickle, but found her green gown instead, and after first using it to wipe the dust from a string of peppers, hung it in the doorway to air. "Where did he say he came from," she asked, "this angel of yours?"

"His home," said Penrhyd, "is in heaven."

"Ah well," said Granni, shaking out the green linen folds, "there are many mysteries known only to the Arch Druids, of whom my grandfather was one, on the maternal side. But for all that, I know what is best for the country. The skies are full of birds; it is scarcely safe any more to sit out under a tree. The last thing we need up there are angels."

Unable to find the sickle, she drew out a necklace of blue beads and hung it about Penrhyd's neck. "If only you could do the Carthaginian dance," she said, and sighed.

"I will try to learn it," said Penrhyd, "if that would please you."

"You are a good child," said Granni, "and I will do something for you, too, one of these days."

The bad weather kept up; at night all Britain lay dark and silent under the rain, only a few lights shining in all the leagues of forest and marsh. The duns of the chieftains, the fortressed keeps of the princes, the Saxon home-burgs were shuttered tight, only a lantern here and there swung its dim circle of light through the wet, flying darkness.

And then one night, no different from the others except for a meal of mushrooms which Granni cooked for her, Penrhyd went to her pallet, said her prayers, turned on her side, and slept, and dreamed.

She dreamed that she was gone to visit her mother in Ireland. Granni, like a great bird, flew her on her back across the drenched, black forests, and over the sleeping mountains to the sea, and there left her, first giving her as a parting gift a sprig of mistletoe and a little bag of rosemary. "You will know what to do with the rosemary," she told her, "when the time comes; but on no account loose the mistletoe from your hand." With that she vanished, a darker shadow among the black shadows of the night.

At the shore, gently bobbing in the waves, Penrhyd found a small curragh waiting for her, which, as she stepped into it, started of its own accord across the water. As it sped her westward, laughing sea creatures frolicked about the little vessel, which seemed drawn onward by a mysterious force. One of them, like a small bear, floated upon its back, while opening oysters which it offered Penrhyd to eat. She thanked the creature, and it replied in Gaelic.

The sun rose, the sky filled with the most beautiful shades of rose and amethyst, and the curragh grounded gently on the shore. Ireland was all in misty colors of green, with flowers in the meadows and birds singing in every tree. She saw her mother's palace from afar, shining in the silver light, and ran toward it; but as she came nearer the scene changed, the palace disappeared, and she found herself on a desolate plain surrounded by brooding mountains, and in the center of it a great barrow of the dead. While she watched, the barrow opened, and there came out a great number of kings and queens and warriors wearing breastplates and shoulder cloaks of gold and with golden ornaments in their hair and on their arms; and as they stepped out onto the ground, small, dark people came out of the woods and entered the barrow in their place.

She knew that her mother was at her side, although she could not see her. "Give me your rosemary for remembrance," said her mother, "for I have forgotten the sound of life, and where I am there are no sweet herbs or fragrance of honeysuckle at night." Penrhyd handed her the little bag of rosemary, and her mother took it.

"Come," said her mother; "it is time to go"; and taking her by the hand, led her toward the barrow. But at her first step the air grew cold around her, and by the side of a darkly flowing river she hesitated and drew back. "Are you not coming with me?" asked her mother sadly.

As she stood there, troubled and uncertain, she saw Thomas of Glen Daur in the middle of the stream, with harebells in his hands. "Now I shall have blue flowers for my hair," she cried, and held out her arms to him, but he shook his head. "They are for the women of Barbary," he said, "who wear hoops of gold in their ears."

Weeping, she saw a kingly procession winding down from the mountains, and her mother beside a great King of Ireland, but when she called out to her, she did not answer, and the procession entered the barrow and was lost to sight. "You do not need me after all," said Thomas from the water. "How can you say that?" she cried, "when you know it is not true?"

Striving to reach his hand which held the flowers, she leaned far out upon the stream, and fell. . . .

And woke, drenched to the skin, to find Granni standing over her, holding an empty water jar. "My mother is dead," she said, "and has forgotten me. She would have had me stay with her."

"I know," said Granni, "and for that reason I gave you the sprig of mistletoe, to keep you from harm." And bending over, she took what she thought was the mistletoe from Penrhyd's grasp.

But when she went to look at it, she saw that she held a little bunch of harebells in her hand.

CHAPTER 15

The small band of Saxon raiders, holed up in a burned-out farmstead at the edge of the fens and marshes east of Tavistock, were heartily sick of watching the rain, playing at knuckle-bones, listening to one of their number recite bits of the Niebelungen Lied, and singing about the Tannenbaum, the fir tree of their native forests. "One should never go anywhere without women," said Sigurd, a red-faced young man with a large mustache; "even that girl that Wulfie found would have been a comfort to have around, although she did not inspire me with mother-confidence." "I would as lief go to bed with a peeled stick," said an old warrior named Otto, "as with a green maiden weighing less than a firkin of ale." "She could nevertheless have cooked us something besides fried beef every day," said Sigurd. "Well, there you have it," declared his friend Rudi: "our Wulfie has to give her a slap sends her tumbling to the ground." "A woman does not talk back to a man," said Wulfram sulkily, "without she gets a slap."

At the end of a week their supply of mead was running low, and the men were beginning to grumble openly. Several quarrels developed, which Otto, the leader, was barely able to settle before the quarrelers had split each other's skulls open; and forays into the rain-drenched countryside in search of a neighboring farm or hamlet turned up nothing except empty marshes and desolate woods. However, on the eighth day, a thrall, who spoke some Saxon from having been married to a Saxon serving wench, happening to pass by the farmstead with a hogshead of metheglin from his master, Erchenwyn of the East Seaxe, as a small gift to Cador of Isca, the companions were able to replenish their carrying jars, and learned, besides, of a Fair to the west of them, on the high moors south of Malmesbury, where there was not only plenty to eat and drink but booths of gold and silver, beads, copper and bronze ornaments, and Carthaginian dancers. "We could return to the West Seaxe as rich men," said Otto thoughtfully, "with golden earl-bands on our arms." "Washael!" cried Sigurd, lifting his drinking horn, only to put it down again in disgust. "This damned weather!" he said. "There is water in it."

But the rains ended at last, the skies lightened, clouds trailed their watery shadows across the hills in the ragged sunshine, and the little band of Saxon warriors, led by Otto, set out from their uncomfortable bivouac in the ruined farmhouse and headed west. Mist rose from the fens steaming in the sun, and bitterns were booming in the marshes—"Like our Saxon war horns," said Sigurd happily. To this Rudi replied: "There will be many battles yet before we win this land for our own." "I have often thought," said Sigurd, "how fortunate that it was here, else where would we have gone? We would have had nowhere to go."

"Just the same," said Wulfie suddenly, as they rode toward higher ground, "I would like to find that girl again that I gave the slap to." This remark was greeted with shouts of mirth from his companions. "What?" cried Rudi. "I thought you did not care for her!" "It is not so much a caring," said Wulfie sheepishly, "as a kind of surprise." "What kind of a surprise is that?" asked Otto, puzzled. "It is a surprise," said Wulfie, "that I should think about her so much." "You gave her a proper slap," said Rudi, "and left her on the ground like a broken stick." "So I did," asserted Wulfie, "and she deserved it. But she left me a heart pain." "Sa!" said Otto, making the ancient sign to ward off evil. "She must have been a witch, and she has put a death on you!" "Ak!" said Wulfie. "What a gray-looking way to die!"

At the same time that the raiders were picking their way westward, a smaller cavalcade was leaving Isca bound north across the high moors toward the Great Meadow and Malmesbury. They went slowly, for their plans were unformed, their destination uncertain, and Azael was troubled by the thought that he had failed in his profession, not once but twice, in allowing Penrhyd to be taken from him and for rushing off to rescue her without waiting for word from On High. Yet he was inclined, despite a natural humility, to blame the others too: Nicias for engaging him in philosophical arguments and thereby diverting his attention from his true business, and Thomas for not staying close enough to Penrhyd to protect her. But most of all he blamed himself. "I should have known," he said, "that if the child was taken, it was with God's knowledge; and that when He is ready He will lead us to her again, and not before." And he reflected bitterly on the picture he must have presented to his superiors. "How Michael must have laughed," he thought, "to see me rushing off to challenge the entire Saxon host with a dagger, an inkhorn, a slingshot, and a featherbed!"

Except that Michael never laughed. No angel
ever did.

And when Thomas begged him to move a little
faster, he refused. "Do not," he admonished him,
"ask me to tempt heaven once again. Whatever
the Lady Penrhyd's fate, she is in God's hands,
which we must believe or be no better than
Ammonites." "The saints forbid!" exclaimed Odo
in pious horror, although he did not recognize
the name, and thought it another heresy like those
which plagued the Church at that time. "Well,
then," said Thomas bitterly, "in that case, God's
hands must have blond hairs on them." "Tut, tut,"
Odo reproved him; "that is fine talk for a Christian!" But Nicias interposed calmly: "The gods
take on the form and coloring of those who worship them; otherwise they would not be recog-
nizable. When Athene, a fair-haired Hellene, became Minerva, she was pictured as a Roman matron; yet they were one and the same, alike in
wisdom and social position. The Saxons worship
Woden, who has blond hair on his hands; yet according to our friend Odo, the One he worships

[173]

and calls God is Lord of all, including both those with brown hair and those with gold." "Do not forget black," whispered Dame Margit with a self-conscious glance at Azael.

Addressing himself directly to the Abbot of Swynneddfod, Nicias continued: "Let us suppose that you are right, and that there is but a single Deity, infinite and indivisible, just and omniscient. In that case, I should like to ask you if you are aware of the great number of heresies with which His Church is confronted: Ebionitism Elkesaitism, Gnosticism, Neo-Platonism, Sabellianism, Chiliasm, Montanism, the Miletian Schism, the Paschal Controversy, Manicheanism, the Arian, Nestorian, and Apollinarian heresies, and the influence of Pelagius? These are not all, but they are all that I have encountered in my studies." "It is indeed a Devil's broth of confusion," Odo agreed, "and it would take a Doctor like Jerome or Basil to skim it." "Perhaps our friend Azael would oblige," said Nicias.

But Azael refused to be drawn into a purely theological discussion. "Frankly," he said, "I am not very learned in matters of orthodoxy, and have not given the problem much attention. I am concerned by something else. In the past, I never had any trouble because of my skin; I was accepted in Sodom and in Jerusalem without comment. When Sheba came from Ethiopia to visit Solomon, all Israel rejoiced. I was not asked to sit below the salt in Thebes, which we called No-Amon, where I watched over Joseph; or at the court of Artaxerxes, to which I accompanied Esther. Am I to believe that God, our heavenly Father, did not know what would happen to His colored children? Is it possible that His Omniscience failed to foresee their present situation?"

"Such a thought is out of the question," said Odo. "I am glad to hear you say so," said Azael. "So it must be that I, personally, am at fault."

And bowing his head, he humbly asked forgiveness, although he was not exactly sure what he had done.

As they rode on through the fresh-smelling, shadowy forest, and forded the little streams in spate after the downpour, he continued to express his thoughts, which were troubled and melancholy. "I no longer feel at home in the world," he admitted, "for it is not a simple place any more. I wonder sometimes if God knows how complicated it has become. Wars alone do not disturb me, I am used to them. But they were wars for the possession of a well, or a city. Is it possible that someday men will battle for an idea? This is something new in the world; and it has only just occurred to me, after hearing Prince Cador remark that he would not care to be taken to heaven by a colored angel."

The old Roman road, its ruts filled with rain water, and overgrown with furze and brambles, rose from the forests and marshes to the upland screes, and led north across the great heath of Dartmoor. The heath lay around them as far as eye could see, a bleak wilderness of gray rock with patches of scrub at the foot of granite tors, massive and terrible. No birds sang, although wedges of wild geese flew overhead, and ravens perched on the low branches, watching the travelers as they passed. On those high moors the wind was never still, but moved in great tides above them, as silent as the clouds which trailed their shadows over the gray land and the gray stones. "It is a strange thing," said Odo, "but the higher I climb toward heaven, the less I feel secure. In this I am the opposite of Brother Elias, who is happiest when perched on a pillar thirty feet in the air." "That is because he has lifted himself above the earth," said Nicias, "in a single thrust, like a tree or a flower; whereas in our case we have followed the road upward into the forbidden realm of the gods. Here, we think, we are very close to the thunderbolts; and we are right. One has to be a philosopher to survive under such conditions." "I do not want to be hit by a thunderbolt," said Godwin, beginning to cry; but Thomas, brandishing his sword, declared that he was not prepared to die until he had rescued Penrhyd from her fate. "If you do," said Dame Margit acidly, "she will have nowhere to sleep, now that you have taken her featherbed."

Two red deer, a doe and a fawn, came out of a thicket by the roadside, and seeing the travelers, stopped and stared, ears up and nostrils quivering. Recognizing Azael, the mother nudged her fawn, and both animals thereupon knelt amidst the broom, while Odo raised his pectoral cross and blessed them. He then rode up abreast of Nicias and remarked:

"Can one doubt the divinity of the Lord, or of his servant, when even the animals do reverence?" "Quite so," replied Nicias, unimpressed, "but the stag, the wolf, the bear, and the peccary have also been known to kneel to Diana, who was called Artemis by the Greeks." "She was not black," said Odo heatedly, "and besides, she was a woman." "The Artemis of Crete," said Nicias, "who was known as Britomartis, or Dictynna, was generally considered to be black, when worshipped in certain islands of the Sporades." "I am glad to hear that," said Azael, coming up beside them, "even though it is a fact that Diana, or Artemis, does not exist." "I would be interested to hear her reply to that observation," remarked Nicias, "although I should prefer not to be present when she makes it." "There is only one God," said Azael, out of patience, "whose Name cannot be uttered even by the angels."

As he spoke, thunder rumbled on the horizon, and hail fell although there were no clouds overhead. "You may be right," said Nicias hurriedly.

"On the other hand," he added uncertainly a moment later, "it could have been Diana."

While Odo sang a quiet Laudamus, they descended into the forest again and took the direction of Malmesbury and the Great Meadow.

CHAPTER 16

Under the warm sun and the gentle, cloud-flecked sky, the Fair at the Great Meadow, which had of necessity been shut down for the rains, was again attracting its dozens of visitors. Dressed in the round woolen caps of pre-Roman days, long cloaks of tartan, and knee-length kirtles, the free-men and farmers, charcoal-burners, bird-catchers, drovers, shepherds, and millers, wandered up and down between the booths, admiring the colorful displays, or gathered in front of the animal cages, and cast sly glances at the women in their short-sleeved jackets and skirts of woven cloth or corded fringe just below the knee. The wizards and necromancers had hung out their signs, and gipsy girls danced in front of their tents, their wide skirts flaring, and their gold anklets, bracelets, and earrings making a tinkling sound among the loud voices, shouts, laughter, haggling of merchants, and shuffling of feet.

The sign in front of one such booth, built of withies and covered with a gaily colored cloth, read:

Granni, Dr'ss. Est. 534.
Auspices, Auguries, Hand and Palm Readings.

Bowl and Stones . . . *1 penny.*
Toad . . . *2 pd.*
Chicken
Heart and Liver . . . *3 denarii.*
Full Intes. . . . *4 skeatta.*
Spotted Bull . . . *2 gold pcs.*

The dancing girl drawing attention to this sign was slim and gray-eyed, and the movements of her dance were performed with an air of propriety which gave them an unexpected piquancy. Several farm wives allowed their husbands to stand for a moment watching, before pulling them away to visit the booths of the goldsmiths, bronzeworkers, perfumers, potters, and dealers in ribbons and notions.

Penrhyd was not unhappy, although she did not like to be stared at, and was embarrassed by the golden hoops in her ears. She was glad to help Granni, who had rescued her from the forest and had taught her so many domestic skills.

A drover from the north country of the Brigantes, having sold three oxen for a good price to a farmer from south of the Exe, stopped for a moment to watch, and then, encouraged by Penrhyd's youthful appearance, stepped into the booth to have his fortune told. He found the Druidess seated before a table of polished fruitwood, on which she had placed a cage containing a fowl, a flat butchering stone, a bronze knife, a bowl of water, two pebbles, and a bag of toads. A round hearthfire was burning in the center of the booth, beneath a copper cauldron in which masses of savory herbs were simmering. "How much do you wish to spend?" asked Granni, motioning him to a seat across from her. "A penny? Or a gold piece?"

"Well, then, neither one," said the drover. "I could go for more than a penny, but a gold piece is beyond my means." "In the old days," said Granni, "my ancestors minted their own gold pieces. Perhaps you have seen one, with the head of Cunobelin engraved upon it? No? Well, no matter. One could be proud to be a Briton in those days." "Are you not proud now, ma'am?" asked the drover anxiously. "I have had no reason to be proud since Badon Hill," said Granni morosely. "And what was that, ma'am," asked the drover, "if I may be so bold?" "It was a great victory," said Granni, "for Prince Arthur." But the drover apparently had never heard of him. "He was High King of Britain," said Granni. "Ah," said the drover, "there were many kings of Britain." "He was married to Gwenifer," said Granni. "Now I remember him," said the drover; "the poor sod."

As the morning drew on, others came to have

their fortunes told and to ask for omens of the future. Several toads were sacrificed, and the fowl slain and disemboweled, and its heart and liver studied for signs and portents. One well-to-do farmer and his wife bought the fire augury, which obliged Granni to lick the edge of her bronze dagger heated by a rowan-tree faggot, and for which she charged five silver pieces. But no one could afford the spotted bull, which was fortunate, since she had no such animal ready, although, as she explained to Penrhyd, she knew where she could lay her hands on one if she had to. "I do what I can to follow the old ways," she said, "and to keep alive the customs and traditions of my ancestors. Perhaps it does not seem like much; but if Britain is to survive, it will be because of people like myself, who know who their grandparents were."

At noon they stopped for a bite of cheese and a herring, and Granni sent Penrhyd down to the animal cages to buy a hen, or, failing that, a bird of any kind suitable for divination. "A dove would do," she said, "or a goose, or even a plump robin, which we could dye a proper color to look like a squab. But do not come back with anything very large, for I do not have room in the booth for many more intestines."

Penrhyd skipped down the midway in the bright noon sunshine, examining with delight the various counters piled high with colored silks and shining brooches and rings of bronze, silver, and gold. But her main curiosity was reserved for the dancing girls in their flounced dresses. "So this is what men like in a woman," she told herself, "and to such they give bouquets of flowers."

But at the animal cages, seeing the keepers with their black African faces, she was reminded of Azael, and burst into tears. And when she heard that Azael had indeed passed that way in search of her, she wept afresh, though whether from joy or sorrow she did not know. "Dear angel," she cried, "surely you will find me now!" But when she tried to bring his face to mind, the only features she saw were those of Thomas of Glen Daur.

Since there were no birds to be found among the animal cages, she returned to Granni with a young pullet bought from a farm woman, and the two of them took up their separate tasks for the

afternoon, Penrhyd in front of the booth and
Granni inside. The sun shone, the flags and pennants flew, the tests of strength and skill at the
end of the Midway attracted the young men and
the boys, and the sounds of wood hitting wood
and the clang of iron on iron, the happy shouts
of the winners and the excited squeals of the
women, floated out on the air toward the encir-
cling forest and those who approached, concealed
within its shadows.

Penrhyd, doing her sedate little dance which
she imagined to be Carthaginian in its movements,
was unaware of the arrival of the small band of
travelers at the far end of the Fair grounds. It was
already minus two of its members, for Godwin
had received permission to leave the party in order to scout the woods at the edge of the meadow,
which Azael thought safe enough, seeing that
they were so close to the Fair. "Perhaps you will
bring us a squirrel or a hare for our supper," said
Odo hopefully. "Yes indeed," said Godwin, "and
if I meet a wolf or a basilisk, I will kill it." "Oh my
poor lamb!" cried Dame Margit, "I had better
go with you." "To tell the truth," Azael agreed, "I

would be more comfortable in my mind if you were to do so." "Do I have to take her?" asked Godwin piteously, to which Azael replied that Dame Margit would be very useful as a messenger in case he had any message he wished to send. "All right, then," said Godwin without enthusiasm, "come along; but mind you do not make any noise." "Oh no, dearie," his nurse assured him, "I shall be as quiet as a mouse."

So saying, she dismounted, and pinning up her petticoats so as not to impede her movements, followed Godwin into the bushes.

Arrived at the Fair, the remaining members of the party took leave of one another, Azael to visit the animal keepers again, and Nicias and Odo going off in search of food and a shelter for the night. Thomas, who found himself with nothing to do, wandered idly along the Midway, pausing here and there to admire the wares set out by the merchants, and casting sidelong glances from time to time at the dancing girls in front of the booths of the fortune-tellers. There was a larger crowd than usual gathered in front of one such booth, and elbowing his way between the onlookers, he found that they were watching the performance of a young woman whose flashing earrings and whirling skirts drew a number of complimentary, if coarse, remarks from the men. Her back was to him, and he did not recognize the bare midriff she turned toward him; it was not until she spun around in her dance so as to face him that he saw who she was, and felt as though he had been suddenly struck by a club, and was unable to believe it.

As for Penrhyd, the last person in the world she expected to see gawking up at her was Thomas of Glen Daur. In her surprise, she stood stock still, and stared at him with her mouth open. "Well!" she managed to gasp out at last. "Oh my!"

There is a moment when a man's arms must go out to a woman, and hers to him, without any explanation. At such times the only language should be the language of the heart, which says "I love you." Unfortunately the first words that Thomas spoke were quite different. "What in heaven's name are you doing?" he demanded.

His tone was no more fortunate than his

words. Penrhyd's face, which had first turned pale and then had flushed to a rosy glow, turned pale again; and her eyes, which had been so warmly shining, gleamed with the beginning of tears. For a moment or two she stood without speaking; then she swallowed something, possibly her heart. "Well," she said coldly, "so there you are at last."

The crowd which had been enjoying Penrhyd's dance, which it found all the more exciting for its modesty, now turned its attention to Thomas, eyeing him with disfavor; and several uncomplimentary remarks were made. "Sa," declared one beefy individual, "'ee be here; and us could do wi'outen 'ee." But seeing Thomas reach for his sword, he thought better of it, and drew back. "Coom awa' lads," he said, "and leave 'ee to quarrel wi' 'ee sister or sweetheart or whatever. There's better sport elsewhere." So saying, he moved away, and the crowd followed him, leaving the two young people to face each other alone.

They could not think of anything to say. Torn between joy and reproach, rapture and indignation, they stood and stared at each other with flushed and hostile faces. "I must say," said Thomas at last, "I scarcely thought to find you in such a condition." "Indeed?" asked Penrhyd coldly. "Perhaps you did not expect to find me at all." "That is unjust!" cried Thomas bitterly. "For I have been searching for you this entire fortnight, and Odo and Azael too."

Her heart leaped a little in her breast when she heard this, but she did not allow it to soften her. "Well," she said, "I was rescued, but no thanks to you." "You would not have needed rescue," said Thomas, "if you had behaved more modestly." "Oho," exclaimed Penrhyd, "so now it was my fault!" "Did you not ride out, unaccompanied, with an older man," demanded Thomas, "of no kin to you? And so was taken, as Azael said, by God's command." "I'll not believe he ever said anything of the kind!" cried Penrhyd indignantly.

"Besides," she said a moment later, "if I was unaccompanied, it was because my squire"—she spat out the word—"rode too lazily behind me." "I did the best I could," said Thomas. "Well, then," said Penrhyd, "so did I."

"Was the best you could do," asked Thomas, "to

end as a dancing girl at a Fair, with gold hoops
in your ears?" "You liked such women once," said
Penrhyd, "or so you said; you thought them
handsome. Or have you forgotten? With flowers in their hair . . ." "It will be a long time," said
Thomas, "before I tell anyone such stories again."
"It will be a long time," said Penrhyd, "before
anyone asks you."

In their hurt and grievance they failed to hear
the commotion at the farther end of the field, as
Godwin came running for his life with Dame Margit puffing at his heels. "Saxons!" cried Godwin
with what little breath he had left. "There are Saxons in the woods! A whole army hidden in the
trees!"

At once all within earshot fell into panic, the
women turned pale, the men threw down their
beer jars and looked to right and left, wondering
which way to run. For all they knew, they were
surrounded, and there was nowhere to run to, and
no escape. Husbands embraced their wives and
sweethearts, and vowed to die bravely, but with
little enthusiasm; and the women, seeing themselves already prizes of war, closed their eyes in

anguish or stared fixedly at nothing. A few, being Christian, knelt in prayer in front of Odo, who, like one of the Saints of old, stood his ground and blessed everybody.

CHAPTER 17

The Saxons were encamped in the woods beyond
the moor, in a small forest glade surrounded by
great trees and heavy scrub. They were in no
hurry; Rudi had brought down a fat red deer,
and there was enough mead left in the leather
firkins to fill the drinking horns. "The best time
for enjoyment," said Otto, "is before a raid like
this one, where there will not be too much fighting, and where you can sit and think about all

the good things that are going to happen to you. It is not like a battle, where the nice time is afterwards, providing you are still there." "Or if you are dead," declared Wulfie, "what does it matter? Since you are in Walhal, with a girl on your knee." "After tomorrow," promised Otto, "you will have girls on both knees." "Washael!" cried Rudi, lifting his drinking horn to his lips; and "Sieghael!" cried the others, following his example.

When the Saxons did not immediately attack, the panic at the Fair subsided to some extent, and a meeting was called to consider ways and means, and to elect a leader. Odo, as a Church-man of high rank, addressed the company. Stand-ing upon a wooden platform from which the cata-pult, used to test the length of flight of a round stone, had been removed, the holy man exclaimed:

"In this hour of peril and perplexity, let us turn to God, Who will lead us out of the ring of our enemies, and into green and pleasant fields. *Lau-damus te qui in gloriam venit.*"

Gazing about him with a proud and venerable look, he continued: "We are fortunate to have with us someone who was present at many of the important battles of history. Let us elect Azael to be our leader, and follow him to victory."

He was astonished to find the nomination of Azael opposed by Granni, who spoke up from her place in the forefront of the crowd. "The greatest general in the world," she said, "was a woman. I am speaking of my ancestress, Boadicea, Queen of the Iceni, who captured Camulodunum and Londinium from the Romans, and slaughtered seventy thousand." At once voices of protest were heard from the men, many of whom shook their sticks angrily in the air. "I'll na follow a woman," said one burly farmer, "be she never so slaughterous!" "I think I know what is best for the country," said Granni, but she was soon hustled to the rear.

With the Druidess out of the way, Azael was chosen by acclamation, despite his dark skin. He then appointed several lieutenants to help him: Nicias to be in charge of ballistics, by which he meant the stone-throwing catapult, Thomas to head the cavalry, and Dame Margit to serve as quartermaster. But when he asked the head animal keeper to supply the transport, he received a disdainful reply. "Where is the equality?" asked the head keeper. "There are four of us; I should be at least a general like yourself." "I know that your desire is to be superior," answered Azael calmly, "but it does not do to be in too great a hurry about it. It takes a long time. The Jews were chosen by God Himself more than two thousand years ago, and they are still waiting.

"However," he added encouragingly, "you will be in the first line of attack." "In that case," said the keeper happily, "I will sharpen my elephant goad."

Nevertheless, as the day drew on toward evening, Azael grew more and more despondent, and at last confessed to his lieutenants an uneasiness which he could no longer hide. "Frankly, my friends," he admitted, "I am at a loss to know whether to attack or to defend. Our forces are so few that either course seems doomed to failure. And what troubles me most of all is the conviction that the fault lies within my own nature, which was made to be without passion, except for sing-

ing and doing my duty." "Your duty is clear," said
Nicias: "it is to save us from becoming thralls to
the barbarians." "That is obvious," said Azael,
"but what is to guide me?" "Reason is our guide,"
said Nicias; "what accords with it is pleasing to
God; perfect trust must be placed in Providence."
"I wish you would not keep quoting Epictetus to
me," said Azael peevishly.

"With all due respect to our friend Nicias," said
Odo, "he still has not drawn up a plan of battle.
I have been thinking; and I remember how Gid-
eon discomforted the Midianites at the Well of
Harod. He had but a handful, opposed to a host,
but the victory was his, with God's help." And
turning to Azael, he inquired: "Were you not there?
And do you not remember how it was done?"

The angel's dark face lightened, and he clapped
a hand to his forehead. "How could I have forgotten?" he exclaimed. And embracing Odo, he
murmured:

"Oh, brother!"

And calling for Godwin, he dispatched him
with a message for Granni. "Tell her," he said, "to

bring out the spotted bull. Naturally, I do not believe in Druid spells, but we need all the help we can get."

The sun sank slowly in the west as Azael made his arrangements and explained to the men of his command what he expected them to do. The long twilight set in; and in the fading, luminous sky, the last flight of widgeon went wavering by, and bats dipped and wheeled in the blue-misty air. At Azael's order, torches and fat lamps were lighted in front of the booths and the evening business of the Fair was made to continue as though nothing had happened, although many anxious looks were cast at the dark line of trees beyond the meadow's crest. It seemed to Odo, breathing the sweet air, that the light of heaven itself was shining down through the ice-green evening sky, and he recited a quiet prayer in praise of the world which was so beautiful. Then he joined Azael at the animal cages, and with an air of confidence mounted to the back of the great elephant to which he had been assigned.

Looking around him from his lofty perch, he

surveyed the little army which was about to do battle with the Saxons; and seeing Thomas mounted upon a wyvern, he waved encouragement to him. "Good fortune to you, Thomas of Glen Daur," he said, "and may you return victorious this day." "I do not care whether I return or not," said Thomas, "for I have nothing to come back to." And he added disconsolately:

"The Lady Penrhyd has become a dancing girl."

"I did not know that you had seen her," said Odo in surprise. "She is here," replied Thomas, "performing in front of the booth of the Druidess." "Ah, well," said Odo, "I am glad that she has been found; but she must not neglect her studies."

Azael now approached the unicorn, which knelt humbly to receive him upon its back. Rising, it bore him to the front of the army, which consisted of the four keepers, the catapult bearing Nicias and drawn by a bear, Thomas upon the wyvern, and several stout yeomen and farmers, among whom Dame Margit was busily distributing candles hidden within pottery pitchers, and small horns and noise-makers taken from the merchants' booths, while Godwin, unnoticed, and clutching his slingshot, crept up behind Odo's elephant and took hold of its tail.

Seated on his fierce unicorn, or monoceros, Azael reviewed his troops. "Friends," he said, "companions, and fellow soldiers: the maneuver upon which we are engaged has only been seen on earth once before, at which time it was successful beyond anyone's hopes. Let us hope that we shall be equally successful. However, I must warn you that the timing must be exact, and you must pay strict attention to every detail. We must move very quietly, for the essence of the plan lies in maintaining the strictest secrecy, and being able to surprise the enemy. So, then—forward! Light your candles, but keep them hidden within your pitchers; and when you hear me cry 'The Sword of Gideon!' do what you have to do, and what has been explained to you."

Giving the signal to advance, he moved forward toward the forest, followed by Thomas on the wyvern, Odo upon the elephant with Godwin clinging to its tail, and Nicias mounted upon the catapult.

The Saxon encampment was easily discovered, for the raiders had built a huge fire of brushwood, around which they were gathered, singing their Saxon songs, while the firkins were emptied one by one and the drinking horns passed from hand to hand. "I am glad we have this fire," said Wulfie, "for I had a dream that a great Troll came out of the forest and devoured us all." "That was not one of our Trolls," said Rudi, "but a Cymric witch who wants your blood." "Do not joke about a matter like that," said Wulfie; "blood is a very serious thing." "Well," said Rudi, "we will get you some extra tomorrow."

In the dark, Azael disposed of his forces in a wide arc, each man at some distance from his neighbor, with his horn or noise-maker in his right hand and the pitcher concealing the lighted candle in his left. When he felt that the moment had come and that the camp was entirely surrounded, Azael gave the signal; and every man broke his pitcher, and blew his horn to make as loud a noise as possible, while Nicias released a stone from the catapult into the very middle of the fire, which strewed out sparks in all directions.

The candles glittered in a great circle among the trees, and at the same time the elephant, goaded by its keeper, crashed forward with a terrifying roar, followed by Azael upon the unicorn, and Thomas upon the wyvern.

It was too much for the Saxons, already befuddled by mead, and with Trolls and witches on their minds; the lights, the noise, the sudden appearance of the frightful beasts plunged them into a panic in which they fell over one another in their haste to get away, scrambled onto their horses, which plunged and reared in terror, and dashed blindly off into the night, peppered by stones from Godwin's slingshot, and leaving everything, swords, shields, axes, and javelins, behind.

It was a great victory, the forces of Britain suffering only one casualty. Charging forward at full speed, Thomas's wyvern suddenly stopped and stuck its head into the ground, and Thomas sailed off its back, landing with a thump that knocked him senseless in the middle of a briar patch.

He was borne back to the Fair grounds on a litter made from two Saxon shields, and deposited in front of Granni's booth; and there Penrhyd found him, and knelt beside him, and gazed into his face, which was pale, and scratched with brambles. His eyes were closed; and seeing this, she wept for pity, and love, and shame at the way she had treated him. "Dear Thomas," she whispered, "please do not die, for I am sure I could not bear it."

Opening one eye, Thomas saw that someone had placed a little spray of withered harebells on his tunic; and since they reminded him of the forest stream and the great boar, he gave a groan. At once he was surprised to feel a tear fall upon his face, and looking up, saw that it was Penrhyd bending over him. "I am always falling into something," he murmured weakly. "I do not mind," she said, and bent to kiss him. "Someone once called me a plucker of roses," he said after a while, "and he was right after all, for I am not very brave." "No," she said, "you are not, but perhaps you will become braver." "I was not even brave enough," he said, "to tell you that I did not come on this journey for Sir Anglas's sake, but for yours." "That is what I thought," said Penrhyd, "but I waited for you to say it." "Well, I have said

it," he declared, "but I am not very lighthearted."
"That, too," said Penrhyd bravely, "you will be,
after we are married."

In another part of the Fair grounds, Godwin
also had a few things to say. "After this," he told
Dame Margit, "please do not call me Master Godwin any more. I have been in a battle, where I
put to rout a large force of the enemy, and possibly wounded or even killed several of them." "You
are a great hero, love," said Dame Margit, "but
your hair needs brushing, for there is something
from the elephant in it."

CHAPTER 18

The Lady Penrhyd of Nairn and Thane and
Thomas of Glen Daur were married in Malmesbury
Priory. The Prior Bedwyr himself performed the
ceremony, which was duly inscribed by Brother
Tinian in his History; while the bride was es-
corted to the altar by Odo, Abbot of Swynneddfod, who gave her into the trembling hands of
the groom, whose supporters were Nicias and
Azael. She was dressed in a golden gown and a

[205]

white veil loaned to her for the occasion by Granni, and was followed up the aisle by Dame Margit as matron of honor and her young cousin Godwin as page. On her head, above the veil, she wore the Celtic circlet of yellow Irish gold, a wedding gift of the Druidess, who was observed several times to brush a tear from her eye during the service. After the ceremony, a reception was held at the villa, where the mourning bands had been taken down for the afternoon, and the last of Aurelius's amphorae of Falernian brought up from the wine cellar.

As the time came for the young couple to make their farewells, it could be seen that they were suffering from embarrassment, Penrhyd perhaps more so than Thomas, who nevertheless appeared constrained and even a little morose. The reason was soon made clear, when they came to Azael and did not know what to say. "Dear Azael," said Penrhyd at last, "I owe you all my happiness. But . . ." She hesitated, only to have Thomas finish the sentence for her. "Do you have to come with us?" he demanded unhappily.

The angel bent a regard both loving and sorrowful upon the young woman whose guardian he had been. "Dear child," he said gently, "you no longer need me; if I were to go with you now I should only be intruding where angels have no business. The married life of a man and a woman is not heaven's concern, but their own: it is for them to make joy out of grief, mirth out of sorrow, and light out of darkness. They do not need a guardian angel, for each is the other's guardian, on earth as in heaven."

Penrhyd looked for a long, last time at the dark face and the tall figure which already seemed bathed in a mistier light. "I shall miss you, Azael," she said at last, feeling a weight in her throat. "Will you still be near me? And can I call you, in need?"

He shook his head. "I have been summoned home," he said, "for I am needed at another time and in another land. Where that is, or what it is called, I know no more than you, for it has not been discovered yet; but I believe it to be somewhere beyond the western ocean.

"Farewell, dear child; I leave you in this time, and this place, which are yours. Be happy, and cherish one another, and the world, which in each man's lifetime is made to bloom only once, by kindness and men's love, so far as I know."

Penrhyd's eyes grew misty. "I have never seen your wings," she said, "except in my dream. I wish that I might see them once, before you leave me."

The angel raised his face to heaven, as though in silent prayer; and as he did so, his figure began to grow luminous, and two huge wings, dark as the night sky, rose from his shoulders and spread themselves in a great screen above his head. His face glowed with a terrible beauty and with the light of inexorable law.

And then, suddenly, he was gone.

"A remarkable phenomenon," said Nicias. "I do not think its like is to be found in any of our natural histories."

The Abbot of Swynneddfod took a deep breath. "I knew all along," he said, "that they should not have put him below the salt."

And he added soberly:

"I shall have to think about that."

BOOKS BY

ROBERT NATHAN

Novels

STONECLIFF (*1967*)   THE MALLOT DIARIES (*1965*)

THE FAIR (*1964*)

THE DEVIL WITH LOVE (*1963*)   A STAR IN THE WIND (*1962*)

THE WILDERNESS-STONE (*1961*)

THE COLOR OF EVENING (*1960*)   SO LOVE RETURNS (*1958*)

THE RANCHO OF THE LITTLE LOVES (*1956*)

SIR HENRY (*1955*)   THE TRAIN IN THE MEADOW (*1953*)

THE INNOCENT EVE (*1951*)   THE MARRIED LOOK (*1950*)

THE ADVENTURES OF TAPIOLA (*1950*)
(*containing* JOURNEY OF TAPIOLA, *1938*,
and TAPIOLA'S BRAVE REGIMENT, *1941*)

THE RIVER JOURNEY (*1949*)   LONG AFTER SUMMER (*1948*)

MR. WHITTLE AND THE MORNING STAR (*1947*)

BUT GENTLY DAY (*1943*)   THE SEA-GULL CRY (*1942*)

THEY WENT ON TOGETHER (*1941*)

PORTRAIT OF JENNIE (*1940*)   WINTER IN APRIL (*1938*)

THE BARLY FIELDS (*1938*)
(*containing* THE FIDDLER IN BARLY, *1926*,
THE WOODCUTTER'S HOUSE, *1927*,
THE BISHOP'S WIFE, *1928*, THE ORCHID, *1931*,
and THERE IS ANOTHER HEAVEN, *1929*)

THE ENCHANTED VOYAGE (*1936*)   ROAD OF AGES (*1935*)

ONE MORE SPRING (*1933*)   JONAH (*1925*)

These are BORZOI BOOKS, *published in New York by* ALFRED A. KNOPF

A NOTE ON THE TYPE

THE TEXT of this book is set in CALEDONIA, a Lino-
type face designed by W. A. Dwiggins (1880-1956),
the man responsible for so much that is good in
contemporary book design and typography. Caledonia belongs to the family of printing types called
"modern face" by printers—a term used to mark
the change in style of type-letters that occurred
about 1800. Caledonia borders on the general design of Scotch Modern but is more freely drawn
than that letter.

Composed, printed, and bound by
H. Wolff, New York.